SCINTILLATE

The Spectrum Series

SAMANTHA MINA

SCINTILLATE

PREQUEL TO THE SPECTRUM SERIES

For Daniella, Ginny, Marie and Rachel
to whom my lifeline
is inextricably entwined.

PRONUNCIATION GUIDE

Buird: *"Bird"*
Ichthyosis: *"Ik-thee-OH-sis"*
Lechatelierite: *"Luh-shaht-LEER-ahyt"*
(rhymes with "light")
Nuria: *"NER-ee-ah"*
Qui Tsop: *"Key Sop"*
Xon: *"Shawn"*

Author's Introduction

This book is a result of questions. Questions from curious readers. Why is the Spectrum series about the *Second* War? What made Captain Terminus Lechatelierite—Cease's grandfather—so 'great'? And, what's the deal with Captain Spry Scintillate—Scarlet July's grandfather—whose mysterious legacy contributed to Scarlet's own Circle Trial condemnation?

Burning to answer those questions, I couldn't wait to sit down and churn out a prequel. With *Iridescence* already complete, I looked upon my new project with enthusiasm and relief: I wasn't ready to say goodbye to Second Earth, quite yet!

There are a handful of protagonists in this novel, but the man at the forefront—Spry Scintillate—is a System soldier. Yes, one of the 'bad guys.' So, prepare yourself for the strange desire to sort-of root for the enemy. I hope this will help my readers come to see that war is far murkier than 'us versus them' or 'good versus evil,' as 'enemies' typically see themselves as the heroes of their own stories.

A note on chronology: this book may take place decades before *Spectrum*, but it is meant to be enjoyed after installments one through five. You might find yourself a bit confused if you attempt this novel without any prior knowledge of Second Earth. Also, *Scintillate* gives away a few crucial details about the main series. (In other words: spoiler alert!)

So, to those of you who've already journeyed with me through the terrors and triumphs of the Second War—diving through the cobalt-blue depths of the icy Septentrion Sea and running barefoot across the fiery red-orange Conflagrian desert—I offer my sincerest welcome. Travel with me now to a day and age prior to Scarlet July and Cease Lechatelierite, though not without champions of its own. To those of you who haven't yet followed me into the future, I encourage you to go and do so first, and then come and meet me back here in the past. Don't worry, Spry and Terminus will still be waiting for you. After all, history may be ignored sometimes, but it never really goes away.

~Samantha Mina

NORTHWESTERN HEMISPHERE OF SECOND EARTH

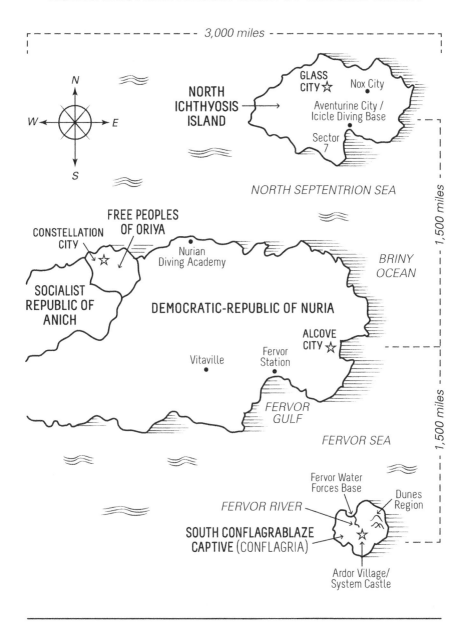

GENEALOGY

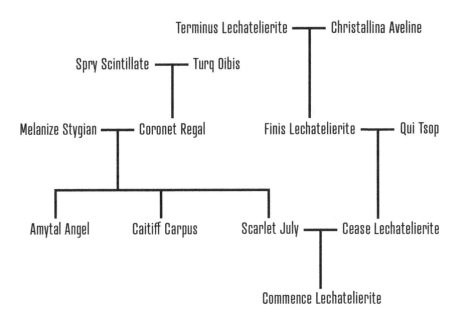

PROLOGUE

It was the seventieth age of Second Earth's sixth era and the Island of Fire was hot with discontentment. For eras, the South Conflagrablaze Captive remained the most isolated of the seven-hundred states of Second Earth. Blacklisted and humiliated, Conflagria despised its status as a so-called 'third-world' country and desperately thirsted for greatness.

By now, Conflagria's population had grown too large for the totalitarian System to quell absolutely and continually; mages could break free from the Core Crystal's spectral thought-control for up to seven minutes at a time. The System initially considered enforcing reproductive restrictions to remedy this, but the idea was ultimately rejected for two reasons. Firstly, the Multi-Source Enchant was still yet to come, and it was assumed that such a law could delay his or her arrival further. Secondly, Conflagria wanted to rise from obscurity in the international arena, a goal to which deliberately stifling manpower ran contrary.

In the hope of strengthening the spectral web and expanding its empire in one fell swoop, the System decided to take after the historical First Earth superpowers, ever the fans of imperialism and colonization. Upon invading other lands, the System wished to carve out new fire pits to plant fragments of the Core Crystal.

The real question was: which country to strike first? For practical purposes, the System dismissed any nation outside the northwestern hemisphere. That left only four options: the Democratic-Republic of Nuria, the Socialist Republic of Anich, the Free Peoples of Oriya and the North Ichthyosis Island.

It was determined that Nuria was far too large and mighty. Conflagria had neither the resources nor the manpower to invade such a massive and prosperous nation. Oriya and Anich were smaller and weaker but were well within Nuria's sphere of influence, as they shared borders.

That left Ichthyosis, ripe for the taking indeed: it was small, geographically isolated, lacking in natural resources and underpopulated. As for establishing mage colonies, Ichthyosis was no meteorological paradise, but the System knew that could be remedied with spectral terraforming via Crystal implantation. And, so, it was decided: Ichthyosis would be Conflagria's preliminary target.

By the early eighties, the Ichthyothian Intelligence Agency (IIA) learned of Conflagria's hostile intentions. There was only one thing preventing the mages from striking, quite yet: the absence of their Multi-Source Enchant. The System didn't want to fight without him.

Ichthyosis, the current Order Authority, had no choice but to also gear up for combat. They didn't know when the Multi-Source Enchant would come around, but they figured that it could be any day, now. The country kept its preparations hidden from the rest of the world, as to evade blacklisting.

Military mobilization was difficult for Ichthyosis. Accustomed to isolation, the masses were ignorant about Conflagrian life and culture, let alone what magical warfare would entail. They hardly had a clue what *any* kind of warfare would entail, beyond the distanced, sanitized, politicized perspectives offered in the study of First Earth history.

But, if there was one trait that summarized the character of the Ichthyothian people, it was: determined. The bitter, inhospitable climate of the ice island had spurned a race of inexorable individuals willing to go any lengths to survive and thrive. They lived in a land of extremes—extreme cold, extreme wind, extreme snowfall—and were likewise willing to take whatever measures necessary, however extreme, to achieve success in the arena of high-tech warfare. And, so, the Childhood Program was erected—a military training system so extreme, it was deemed inhumane by civil rights groups across the nation. But, even the activists knew, in the back of their minds, that there weren't many alternatives available. How else would a society that had never known war become masters of it overnight, as to save their sovereignty?

Raised in proud conviction of the Isolationist Laws, few men were willing to give their lives to the condemnable trade of

war. Few had the heart to do what hadn't
been done before on Second Earth and
serve as soldiers. And, so, the logic behind
the Childhood Program was that warriors
were *born*, not made: an Ichthyothian
would only be willing to commit his mind,
body and soul to fighting if raised apart
from the world's anti-war ideology, in an
entirely new sub-culture. A sub-culture in
which there was no taboo against violence.
A sub-culture in which the outcome of
the upcoming conflict meant absolutely
everything. The kids raised in this program
would believe that war was the purpose of
their lives.

Objections were raised among the program's facilitators. Many worried that the
students raised in such an austere environ-
ment—following the same rigid schedule
seven days a week, eating the same foods,
wearing the same uniforms—would lose
their individuality entirely, consequently
hampering their creativity and ingenuity.
And, so, it was determined that *some* form
of personal physical expression should be
allowed. The amusing conclusion the administrators reached was: hair. The soldiers

would be permitted to wear their hair how-ever they liked.

There weren't many parents standing in line to volunteer their children to the pro-gram. So, the administrators—who now called themselves the 'Trilateral Commit-tee,' after the three newly-minted military branches—initiated a firstborn-son draft, for babies twelve months and younger.

One such child was Terminus Expi-ri Lechatelierite, born in Nox City on the winter solstice of the eighty-seventh age, sixth era. He was abducted into the Diving Fleet only weeks after entering the world, despite his mild proportionate-dwarfism and left-eye blindness. Whenever a new child was brought in, the Trilateral Com-mittee couldn't help but hope they'd finally found the leader they'd been searching for, the one who'd be brilliant enough to defeat the Conflagrian Multi-Source Enchant.

Six months prior, on the summer solstice of the eighty-seventh age, a mage with an astounding silver aura was born to the Is-land of Fire. The System admins, eager for war, believed that he was the answer to their prayer. With a frequency that pierced the very heart of the spectral web itself, his long legs and thick hair brimmed with potential. And, so, all hopes on him were immediately laid. Spry Skii Scintillate was too young to say his first words when the very course of his life was already determined.

PART I
CHILDREN OF HOPE

---

*"Sometimes, war becomes inevitable through
the evils of man…
In the end, there is one thing I am sure of.
No matter a war's outcome,
the soldier never wins."*

—*US Army Captain Andrew Exum*

SPRY SCINTILLATE

I was born on the summer solstice of the eighty-seventh age, a national holiday. It was taken as an omen—a good one—that I came to Second Earth on such a happy day. This is a sign, the System said, that he's the one we've been waiting for.

Rather than being named for my color or prospective powers, as was the norm, I was christened after the fact that my wavelength was particularly 'lively' and my aura 'scintillated,' whatever that meant. Spry Skii Scintillate. My first and middle names were simple and monosyllabic. But, my last name, even I was liable to botch.

I remembered the afternoon, about two ages ago when I was four, when my mother and I went out to fetch our family's fire ration, and the woman ahead of us in line struck up some conversation.

"Handsome son you've got there," she said, grinning beneath a profuse heap of wiry deep-brown hair. There was no wondering what *her* source was.

Shyly, I said nothing.

"Thank you," Mother answered politely.

She looked down at me. "What's your name, kid?"

"Spry," I answered.

"Spy, what?" she insisted, probably confused by the lack of colorful reference. I hadn't had my Circle Trial yet, so the System's prediction about me wasn't public knowledge. But, Mother loved to tell me that, soon, I'd be recognized wherever I went. I'd never need to introduce myself, again.

"Spy Ssssinnnntilayt," I slurred.

She froze for a moment before erupting into laughter, streams of spit issuing from her cracked lips.

That afternoon, I asked Mother what my last name was supposed to mean. She said, 'to emit flashes of light.' Or, in other words, to sparkle.

I felt like a freak. While some silver mages got cool names like Sterling Sword, I was 'Lively Sparkles.' It sounded dumb. I knew not to question the System's choice, though, because the System never made mistakes. Everybody knew that.

"It's a hero's name," Mother would tell me, proudly. "Too great to be limited to a single source or color. You're the fulfillment of the prophecy; it's fitting for your name to transcend the usual customs."

Now, how was I supposed to react to *that?* Growing up hearing that you're meant to save the world. I supposed that most kids in my sandals would be excited and smug. But, I just felt sick and scared.

While some children reached the ripe age of six or seven before their powers were determined via careful spectroscopic examination, others were born with it written on their foreheads. Or, at least, their ears. When Auricle Capitulum—a yellow boy who lived in the heart of Ardor Village, along the Dust Path—was born, it was immediately obvious to the medicine men what his source was. He came into the world pawing his ears and wailing. Even the rustle of clothing was too loud for poor Auricle. So, he cried. But, the sound of his own crying was also too loud for him. So, he cried some more. It was a vicious cycle. Vicious, but necessary. Ear mages had to sustain a certain degree of hearing damage when they were very young, so they could live the rest of their lives as functional human beings. It was a standard right-of-passage, terrible as it was. Auricle's parents probably didn't enjoy watching their child suffer so much every day, but they knew they had to let it happen, lest Auricle meet the same tragic fate as Rea Pinna. Legend had it that Rea Pinna's mother locked him up in a soundproof room his entire life, to protect his hearing. At age thirteen, when he went outside for the first time, he was instantly killed by the sound of his brother's sneezes.

I felt sorry for people like Auricle, not because they spent ages crying at the sound of their own crying, but because sharpened hearing was the extent of their powers. To me, it seemed more like a handicap than an advantage. I imagined it'd be very distracting and overwhelming. In my opinion, if you only got one source in your life, ears were a waste.

Anyway, today, I'd finally get confirmation of my source; it was my sixth birthday, the summer solstice of the ninety-third age, sixth era. I now stood in the center of a ring of seven scrutinizing System administrators, listening to them ponder my 'spectral perplexities.'

"Clearly, his legs bear the strongest concentration of spectrum in his body," said a woman with a wrinkly yellow neck. Like most throat mages, she spoke uncomfortably loudly without really meaning to. I couldn't help but wonder what a single word of hers would do to someone like Auricle. It didn't come as a surprise to me that throat and ear mages hardly ever became friends. "But, there's also an unmistakable cluster of photons in his hair." She touched the silvery mess on my head.

Thus far, I'd always assumed I was a leg mage. One evening last age, when I was upset at my parents for grounding me, I ran twenty consecutive miles to some random village, leapt onto the roof of some random cabin, and hid there for a day and a half.

But, at the same time, Mother always told me that my locks had 'that unmistakable hair-mage texture,' by which she meant that it was particularly wiry, thick and stubborn. Magical hair was supposed to be difficult (or, impossible) to cut... and indeed, by now, I'd been banned by every barber in town. The first time I went to one, at age three, the owner literally threw me out of his shop.

"You'll break my scissors," he grunted, holding up his wooden instruments. "You're a hair mage; just retract the length yourself."

"I'm too young to know what my source is," I whimpered.

"I'm no spectroscoper, but a blind scabrous can tell that you're a hair mage. Go suck up the length if you don't want it so shaggy."

"I'm a leg mage. I can't do that."

His eyes narrowed. "You've already gone grey. Either you're much older than you look, or you're a silver hair mage. Now, get outta my hut." And, with that, he seized my swathe and tossed me outside.

And, now, three ages later, I was hearing the same reasoning yet again, but from the mouth of the yellow-throated System admin: "Why else would a six-age-old go silver? Pekoe, I didn't get *my* first grey hairs until I was forty."

She scuttled over to me, ripped a tuft straight from my scalp (ouch) and went to get it tested by the spectroscopers. In minutes, the results were in: positive. The magical traces were just that—traces. But, they existed; that much couldn't be denied.

I knew what that meant. There was only one conclusion that could be reached now, but I didn't want to hear it—

"He's the Multi-Source Enchant. He's the one we've been waiting for."

The entire circle held its breath. My parents beamed.

"No, you're wrong," I broke the silence, voice squeaky with fear. Everyone stared, shocked. Mother looked about ready to jam her torch in my mouth. Traditionally, neither the examinee nor the examinee's family were permitted to talk during a Circle Trial. The rule was set in place to preserve the neutrality and purity of the System's decision, as family members often came with biases and incorrect pre-conceived notions.

"I-I can't do anything with my hair," I went on, feebly. "I mean, it just… sits there.

I can't swish it around or nothing. But, I can run real fast and jump real high. One time, I ran all day without stopping. I'm a leg mage. But, my hair just sits there."

I expected the yellow woman to angrily shush me. But, to my great surprise, she only smiled and said, "That's because you haven't been trained, yet."

"My legs haven't been trained neither, but I can still run good. That comes easy. But, I can't feel or do nothing with my hair."

A dark-cloaked, goateed System admin stood, brandishing a scroll of parchment. "Ma'am, his blood-spectrum-content is five parts-per-milligram. Though remarkable, that isn't high enough to sustain two full sources. At the very least, the Multi-Source Enchant would need a BSC of seven—"

"And, who are we to say with any certainty what the Multi-Source Enchant would or wouldn't *need?*" she roared. "Have we ever met one before, to definitively know what's high enough? It doesn't matter what research has said in ages past when the miracle itself has crystallized here and now, before our very eyes. This child's hair and legs are both spectral. He's the prophet."

The man's arms folded. "Ma'am, I must insist. Eras of Castle spectroscopy studies support the hypothesis that seven parts-per-milligram is the absolute minimum for—"

"Think of the war, Xon. We'd be fools to overlook the mage likely to become our best warrior."

I ducked my head and covered my face. War. I shivered. I didn't want to go to war. I didn't want to be a warrior. Warriors killed people. I didn't want to hurt anybody.

"Call Principal Pekoe. He'll want to be here for this."

All too soon, the Orange One arrived, dressed in his vivid velvet robe and green bowling hat, to stand before us and proclaim what the entire island waited eras to hear: "The Multi-Source Enchant has come to save magekind."

The only problem was, I really, really couldn't move my hair.

AURICLE CAPITULUM

So, I had the rotten luck to be born on the same day as the Savior of Magekind. It sure made Summer Solstice Day a jolly holiday for me, every age. Heard the sarcasm in my voice? Because, I sure as hell did. I heard everything, all the time, whether I liked it or not.

I was unusually receptive for an adult ear mage. I could even perceive some of what went on in the spectral web—an ability usually lost by the age of four. I could never have 'peace and quiet,' as long as I lived. I didn't even understand what the phrase meant. So-called 'quiet' places, like the System Castle Library, were never actually quiet to me. Everywhere I went, the background noise was incredible. I could never give anything my undivided attention—could never focus on my studies as well as my peers—

because I was always distracted by countless sounds coming from Pekoe knew were. To my teachers, it made me come across as stupid and slow. They just didn't understand how their voices got drowned out by kids shuffling in their seats, whispering, coughing, sneezing, biting nails, rolling scrolls…

Sometimes, my powers were fun. I always got first wind of every piece of gossip to traverse the village, without trying. And, accordingly, no one could ever talk about me behind my back. But, in the end, I decided that gossip-mongering and amnesty from slander weren't worth the social stigma and physical pain associated with being a hypersensitive ear mage.

The System declared me 'Useless' at my Circle Trial when I was seven. Not all ear mages met the same tragic fate. There was a war coming, in which spies would be needed. I'd hoped my hypersensitivity would make me a candidate. Wishful thinking. My broad receptivity meant that I picked up *everything*. Secret agents needed to be able to filter out noise pollution.

So, I was only allowed to attend the Mage Castle until I was ten. A couple ages later, the laws changed so that Uselessness were left completely uneducated, so I supposed that I was lucky to get the schooling I did. I was taught to read, write, recite the skeleton of history and understand basic spectroscopy. Then, it was to the taro fields, for me. I was sentenced to physical labor for eighteen hours a day, every day, even holidays and weekends. I was amongst the dregs of society.

I was a nothing, but Spry Scintillate was something. And, not by virtue of our characters nor deeds nor anything we could control. I was condemned and Scintillate was esteemed because I happened to be born with spectral ears, while he had magical legs *and* hair.

Spry Scintillate and his parents lived in a fancy palace in the suburban outskirts of Ardor Village. I'd never been inside their place, but my friend Verteb Aqua once got the chance, when he was tasked with delivering Scintillate's family twenty sacks of taro for some high-society party that they were throwing. Verteb said that their home was a wonderland, with every inch of the spacious interior elaborately ornamented.

There were marble fireplaces at every turn, lit with dancing blue-white flames.

Soon, though, Scintillate was due to be plucked from his cushy life and sent off to war. This was cause for excitement among the peasantry because we knew that the System would need to choose one of 'our kind' to become Scintillate's personal servant. In other words, it was a chance for a promotion. A chance to live on a nice military base rather than a crappy shack. Most of my fellow field-hands dreamed of being picked. But, me and my five best friends didn't. Pekoe forbid, we didn't worship the man.

Most people celebrated and revered Spry Scintillate. Most folks believed that he would bring honor and glory to the island as he triumphed over the Nordics. Most mages looked at Scintillate's muscular frame and vibrant aura and saw the hero Conflagria had been waiting for.

Some, however, wondered if the prophecy meant something else, entirely. Some thought it predicted that the Multi-Source Enchant would strip Pekoe of his authority and take his place. The System, hoping to bring the former interpretation to fruition rather than the latter, channeled a ton of resources into Scintillate's upbringing and education.

As for me, I didn't really favor one interpretation of the prophecy over another. I figured that it was equally possible for Scintillate to turn out either way: he could love the System for all the attention and amenities they'd lavished upon him, or he could hate them for having orchestrated his every blink and bowel movement since his Circle Trial. Of course, Scintillate knew as well as anyone that the System never made mistakes. But, that didn't mean that the boy couldn't still turn out to be a rotten dragon egg. People didn't always do what was in their best interests, after all. Most children were well aware that consuming entire canes of sugar before dinner was a bad idea, but plenty still did it anyway.

Of course, I wanted Scintillate to pull through. I wasn't stupid. It was in my own best interest—and that of every mage on Second Earth—for Scintillate to succeed. But, just because I wanted him to win the war didn't mean that I longed to wait on him, hand and foot. Pekoe forbid if I was a tiny bit bitter against people like him who had all the luck in this world.

TERMINUS LECHATELIERITE

It was morning. I stood before the locker-room mirror, buttoning my shirt and inspecting my milky-blue iris. I hated how the upper lid hung halfway shut. I would've preferred if it were completely closed. But, I had neither sensation nor control over that entire side of my face. Even my smiles were lopsided. Not that I smiled too often, anyway.

I tipped my head back and squeezed in a couple drops of saline. Because I couldn't close my left eye, I had to moisturize it, several times a day.

Then, peering at my reflection again, I desperately tried to comb my hair back so it'd stay out of my good eye. No matter how much gel I used, it never obeyed.

Adaman Buird, crouching on the floor to tie his boots, smirked and murmured, "Really, Terminus, why don't you just get it cut?"

His own head was shaved down to a brown fuzz. I'd tried the crew-cut before, a few ages ago, before I got bumped up to Adaman's class (I was now ten and he was fourteen). It looked okay for a day or two. Then it started growing, all lumpy and spiky and uneven. Even when it grew a couple more inches, it *still* didn't lie down—it was too wiry and stiff. I soon learned that, unless my hair was at least three inches long, it'd stand upright like soldiers at attention.

Unfortunately, that meant I had no choice but to walk around the academy looking like some sort of shaggy First Earth American hippy from the nineteen-seventies. It was either that or get it re-buzzed practically every other day. Who had time for that?

I wasn't about to explain all this to Adaman. It'd sound silly. Plus, it was none of his business. I snatched my knapsack from my bunk and headed to class without a word.

My first period of the day was Enemy Life and Culture. The teacher, Sergeant Irri, warned us several times a week that Conflagria was liable to declare war on us, any day now. He doubted if our class would be ready in time.

'Weird' was the best word I could use to describe what we learned in that class. No matter how much we studied the Conflagrian social structure, I couldn't understand why the whole ridiculous system didn't fall apart the moment Principal Pekoe sneezed. It seemed all too obvious that their dictatorship—comically named, 'the System'—was both sloppily-run and brazenly corrupt. Which begged the question: why was Conflagria so *stable?* With nearly seven eras of history, Conflagria was the oldest nation on the map, yet it never experienced a single domestic revolution. Not one. Not even a simple sign-waving, crowd-chanting anti-System demonstration in the streets. The masses were completely docile. It was incredible. It defied the laws of human nature.

One day last age, I asked Sergeant Irri about it.

"Believe me, you're not the first to bring this up," he sighed. "Ichthyosis has dozens of political theorists tackling the issue, as we speak."

"Sir, maybe, it's got nothing to do with political theory," I suggested. "I mean, there's nothing rational about any of this. Nothing to theorize. The System is corrupt and the people are flat-out oblivious to it. The answer is… it's impossible."

He blinked. "That doesn't really sound like an answer to me."

My head shook. "No, sir, what I mean is, it may be impossible to find a logical anthropological or political explanation because no social theory could account for the blind submissiveness of an entire population for generations. But, since Conflagria is a *magical* land, maybe the explanation is supernatural. Maybe, we're approaching the question from the wrong angle, entirely. Maybe, we don't need political theorists looking into this, but physicists and astronomers."

"Astronomers?"

"Anyone with knowledge of spectroscopy. Anyone who could analyze the electromagnetic spectrum."

Irri rubbed his stubbly chin, exhaustion in his gaze. "I have neither the rank nor the time to bring such a strange suggestion before the Trilateral Committee."

"But, sir—"

"And, even if a magical explanation were uncovered, it wouldn't do us any good."

What? "Why not, sir?"

He exhaled, heavily. "Because, Lechate-lierite, when it comes to magic… how do I put this?" He rubbed the back of his neck. "It makes no sense. None, at all, to anyone but mages. The supernatural isn't bound by the rational laws of science. It's unpredictable. We can't experiment intelligently with it."

"If mages can make spectrum do what they want, then there's got to be some method to it. Something that can be figured out. It can't just be random. I mean, don't mage kids go to school to learn to use their auras?"

Irri began to grow impatient. "Exactly: *their* auras. It's organic. We Nordics have no spectrum in our blood and therefore no means to access the web."

My mind raced. "Maybe, genetics aren't everything, sir. Maybe, like the mage kids, we could *learn* to—"

Irri held up his hand. "That's enough nonsense for one afternoon."

"But, sir, this could change our entire strategy—"

"Don't talk out of turn, soldier!"

My chin ducked. "I'm sorry, sir."

Silence.

He cleared his throat. "As long as you're still a student, it's moderately acceptable for you to occasionally amuse yourself with such silly notions. But, by the time you graduate into the fleet, you'll be expected to have grasped the difference between fantasy and reality, especially since your name is currently circulating throughout the Trilateral Committee as the foremost candidate for the captaincy."

"Sir?" I breathed.

"That's right. You could lead the first fleet to go to war in Second Earth history. You wouldn't want to blow a chance like that over some crazy talk, now would you?"

Me, Captain of the Diving Fleet. I knew my test scores were at the top of the academy, but I was also half-blind and developmentally-stunted, so I didn't think I stood a real chance.

"No, sir, I wouldn't," I breathed, floating like a sub in the sea.

AURICLE CAPITULUM

I had a few friends in the fields: Verteb
Aqua, Kidni Trician, Apricot Sheath, Tymp
Anum and Xero Clea. A blue spine-mage,
a purple organ-mage, a peach skin-mage,
a red ear-mage and an Infrared. We were
misfits. The 'wrong crowd.' The bottom of
the social pyramid.

Everywhere we looked, we saw institu-
tionalized prejudice. Take the Fire Pit, for
example. By law, Uselesses and Infrareds
had to forfeit their places in line on demand
to 'normal' mages, to ensure that society's
'real contributors' received their rations in a
timely manner. Never mind that so-called
'unskilled' labor was a real contribution to
society. Spry Scintillate wouldn't have had
his fancy dinner last night if some Useless
or Infrared didn't slaughter, clean and cook
his dragon meat.

I wanted the likes of Scintillate to try walking in my sandals. I wanted 'the Icon,' as me and my friends called him, to experience what it felt like to be eternally condemned. To be despised by society no matter what you did or how hard you worked. I knew I'd never be respected, no matter what I did. I'd never be 'good enough.' I had no hope of rising above second class.

Feet dragging, I trudged back to my family's pathetic shack on the Dust Path. It was twenty-three-o'clock and I was returning from a grueling day of work, carrying my measly fire ration. My torch—more like a candle, really—was too feeble to even send a single wisp of smoke into the mud-brown night sky.

I looked up and saw the moons eclipsing. Omega's silver orb smothered Alpha's yellow light.

AULD PHARYNX

It was the summer solstice of the seventh age, seventh era. A national holiday. The biggest festival of all. Most importantly, it was Spry Scintillate's twentieth birthday. From this day forth, Spry would reside at the Fervor Sea Base with his newly-assembled army, the System Water Forces.

Isolation was key, to keep Spry creative and focused. His only extracurricular interactions would be with his new personal servant. Selecting Spry's servant was the collaborative effort of myself—the Chief of Prophetic Affairs—and two others from my department. We didn't exactly have a pretty pool of candidates to choose from, because we couldn't pick anyone who was already substantially contributing to society. In other words, we could only select from among the Uselesses.

For obvious reasons, Spry's servant couldn't be a woman, nor could he be too old. But, of course, there were many other factors to consider besides gender and age. Even with Uselesses, spectral gifts had to be considered. (I used the term 'gifts' here loosely).

"I say we go with an Infrared, to be safe," Xon Follicle said, stroking his black goatee. "Even the most obscure magic could be weaponized, if the wielder gets creative. We don't want to plant a potential threat, right in Spry's quarters."

Ala Pinion folded his arms, white wings twitching. "Not *all* magic can be used offensively. I don't see how an organ or ear mage could do Spry any harm."

"That's because you've never been forced to really think about it," Xon argued, fanning his dark cloak. "But, if enhanced organs or ears were all you had to work with your whole life, you'd probably manage to come up with *some*thing."

"The only things I can come up with are positive," Ala replied. "Organ mages can't fall ill, for example. That means no sick days. Spine mages can lift heavy loads without risk of injury. And, ear-mages…

they could… well, I can't really think of anything ear mages are good for."

"I've got one," I suddenly spoke up. "Sometimes, ear-mages can hear things going on in the spectral web. They can hear when their own strands get plucked by another's poignant thoughts. Occasionally, they can even sense impacts on the frequencies of those to whom they're twined."

Xon's head shook. "You're speaking of ear-mage *infants*. Anyone old enough to be Spry's servant couldn't possibly be *that* sensitive, anymore."

"Except one," I replied. "Auricle Capitulum, a field-hand. He's twenty today, like Spry, but has retained the auditory receptivity of a three-age-old."

Typically, ear-mages were sensitive to all frequencies in the radio spectrum, particularly the 'water hole'—the wavelength range from the twenty-one-centimeter line of hydrogen to the eighteen-centimeter emission line of hydroxide. Ear-mage babies and toddlers, however, could hear roughly five times beyond that window. Though that gave them special access to the spectral web, it made noise-pollution overwhelming.

I rubbed my throat, weighing the pros and cons of potentially installing a hyper-sensitive ear mage in the fulltime service of the Multi-Source Enchant. It'd be an enormous breach of Spry's privacy, that was for sure. Anything Spry murmured under his breath—and, even some of his thoughts—would be overheard.

Which was exactly why Auricle could be the perfect man for the job.

AURICLE CAPITULUM

Falling asleep was always very difficult for me. The sound of my own head moving on my pillow was enough to keep me up for hours. I had to force myself to lie as still as humanly possible, not even wiggling a toe. Even then, things weren't quiet. I still had to contend with the drone of my parents' breathing in the next room and the obnoxious crackling of the living-room fireplace and the pitter-patter of dragons romping in their pens outside...

Knock, knock, knock!

"Auricle!" my dad barked through the wall. "Get it!"

Sighing, I rose from my wicker tarp, eardrums aching already.

"Knock any harder and it'll fall of the hinges," I retorted, thinking it was probably Verteb or Kidni, seeing if I wanted to go throw rotten scabrous eggs at the Icon's palace with them. I yanked the door open.

"Have some respect when speaking to the Chief of Prophetic Affairs, Useless," admonished an elderly yellow-throated woman.

Holy Pekoe.

"I-I'm sorry, ma'am," I piped, bowing deeply.

My heart pounded fiercely against my ribcage when I saw the scroll in her hands. This was it. I was being singled out for execution, I knew it. The nation was about to go to war with the Nordics and the System decided to drop a few deadweights early.

But, wait, why would the Department of Prophetic Affairs be involved in something as insignificant as the disposal of a Useless peasant?

"H-how may I be of s-service to you, tonight?" I babbled, stowing my hands in my pockets so she wouldn't see them trembling.

With a thin-lipped smile, she held out her scroll.

I took it from her and slowly unrolled it; it rattled noisily in my sweaty fingers:

BY ORDER OF THE DEPARTMENT OF
PROPHETIC AFFAIRS:

AURICLE CAPITULUM (EARS, YEL-
LOW) IS HEREBY REASSIGNED TO
THE PRIVATE SERVICE OF WATER
FORCES CAPTAIN SPRY SCINTILLATE
(LEGS, HAIR, SILVER). PLEASE RE-
PORT TO FERVOR SEA BASE IMMEDI-
ATELY.

SIGNED,

Auld Pharynx, Chief of Prophetic Affairs
Ala Pinion, Vice-Chief of Prophetic Affairs
Xon Follicle, Secretary of Prophetic Affairs

I looked up at Auld in disbelief.

"Wake you parents so you may bid them
farewell," she commanded sharply—my eardrums felt as though pierced by an arrowhead.

"F-farewell? I sputtered, resisting the
urge to cover my ears. People tended to get
offended when I did that. They didn't understand that I often heard *better* that way.

"Immediately," she pointed to the scroll,
"means immediately. You're twenty; legally,
I don't *have* to let you speak to them before
taking you away. I'm only allowing it out of
the goodness of my heart."

"Wait, so... I have to go with you... like, right now?" I breathed. "I don't even get to pack my stuff?"

Auld gave the room a scornful scowl. "We'll provide everything you need. Believe me, you'll have no use for any of this... *junk*."

"I work eighteen hours a day, seven days a week, for this *junk*," I answered, acidly.

At once, I felt a severe pang of regret. I couldn't believe I'd say such a thing to a System administrator. I bit down on my tongue until it bled; I could hear the faint popping of the tiny blood vessels. Of course, nothing I owned could compare to the wonders of the System!

"M-ma'am, I'm *so* sorry." I bowed, repeatedly. "I didn't mean to be rude, I just—"

She silenced me with a whack of her staff. I doubled over.

"You should be kissing my feet, for this assignment. You're being invited into the presence of the Multi-Source Enchant. It's an honor for any mage, let alone a *Useless*."

An honor. Right. That was just about the last word I'd use to describe a life of clean ing soiled outhouses and laundering smelly uniforms. I had to spend the rest of my days waiting on the one mage I despised most in the world. What on Pekoe's island did I do to deserve this?

* * *

I was a Useless. Nothing but a hypersensitive ear mage with a crooked spine. But, from the way I was being searched right now, you'd think I was an armed Nordic guerilla or something.

Before I could enter the base, I had to strip naked and endure two hours (and counting) of invasive prodding and poking. It was unbelievably nerve-wracking, not only because I was exposed in front a bunch of strangers but because these strangers all insisted on barking commands as though we were standing half a taro-field apart.

"Turn to the right!" one man now hollered.

"Please," I whimpered, obeying, "not so loud. I'm right next to you."

He jabbed a spectroscope directly in my left ear. I cried out—and, of course, the sound of my own voice added to the chaotic agony of it all.

"He's a weak one," muttered a green hand-mage.

"It's not weakness," I mewled, blinking back tears. "I mean, how'd you like it if I stuck a spear in your palm, or something?"

The millisecond the words left my lips, all seven officers had me face-down on the floor.

"Where is it?" olive-fingers screeched.

"Wh-where's what?" I choked.

"The spear you threatened me with!"

Was he kidding? "I wasn't making a *threat;* it was an analogy! I was trying to explain how much *this* hurts!" I indicated the thing sticking out of my head.

Immediately, the men seized my arms and threw me into an empty cell, barely wide enough to sit down.

"Hey, what's going on?" I rattled the doorknob. I turned around and around, helplessly perusing the four stone walls, searching for a way out—or, at the very least, an explanation for what on earth was going on, here. Did the System really feel threatened by a Useless peasant? Or, was this some sort of test? I didn't have the mind for riddles and puzzles. No one ever said that this job would require any brains. The System had no right to deny me a proper education then demand I think critically.

Then, a few minutes later, I just... forgot why I was angry. I still had no clue why I was being detained but, suddenly, reasons didn't matter so much, anymore.

The door opened.

"Come along," Auld said casually, tossing me a robe.

Wordlessly, I pulled on the robe and followed her through a maze of stone corridors. I'd never seen so much rock and marble before; in my neighborhood, the only building materials we could afford were clay, wood or straw. As we walked, she gave me a general overview of servant protocol. Greet my master with a bow. Don't ask questions. Speak only when spoken to. Answer every command with 'yes, sir.' And, on and on, her harsh voice hammered.

After about fifteen minutes, we suddenly stopped before a grey door that looked identical to the other hundred or so we'd already passed.

"Go on in," she said. "Your master awaits."

I blinked.

She scrunched her brows, reading my mind. "We're at war, Useless. If Fervor were to get invaded by Nordics, how would it help to post big signs indicating our Multi-Source Enchant's location?"

With that, she nodded curtly and stalked away. A wave of despair hit me.

"Ma'am!" I called after her. Surely, I'd receive *some* formal training before being left at Spry Scintillate's door!

She swiveled around. "Yes?"

I gestured helplessly and babbled the first thing I could think of: "I... I don't know my way around the base."

She blinked, slowly and coolly. "You're at the Captain's quarters. You're where you need to be."

"But... um... like... what if he asks me to... I don't know... fetch him some well water, or something?"

"So, what if he does?"

"I have no clue how to get outside from here."

"Just go back where we came from."

Blood churned in my ears. As we walked, I was so preoccupied with nerves that I hadn't really paid attention to where we were going.

Auld stared. "Well, they did say you were slow," she murmured to herself, knowing full well that I'd hear.

My face went hot.

"I'm sorry, Useless," she droned in a rather unapologetic tone, "I'm not used to working with your kind. I forgot about your limited mental capacity." My temples pulsed. "I guess you're just going to have to learn on the job; as much as I'd like to hang around to change your diapers, I have other more important matters to tend to. Now, hurry up and go on in; it's impolite to keep your master waiting." And, with that, she was gone.

I took a deep breath and faced the Multi-Source Enchant's door, scared and infuriated and embarrassed, all at once. I couldn't believe this was my life, now. I couldn't believe that from now on, I'd singularly interact with some high and mighty military tycoon who needed me to do dumb crap for him like bake his tarot root and iron his uniforms, as if he couldn't grow up and do those things himself.

I closed my eyes, took a deep breath and knocked.

"It's open," said a tired, grumpy voice. He didn't sound too pleased to meet me, right now. Great.

I assumed that the large stone door would be rather heavy. So, being rather small and thin myself, I instinctively leaned all my weight into it.

Bad move. Apparently, I'd overestimated the door—or underestimated myself. The massive frame swung with impressive momentum, slamming spectacularly into Scintillate's desk, causing the overhead shelf and all its contents to dump right onto the man's lap.

Holy Pekoe. "I-I'm so sorry, sir!" I breathed, rushing forward to clean up the heap of books, scrolls, spectroscopes, quivers, quills, weird wooden gismos, dirty robes, glass jars and various other unidentified objects. But, before I could clean up so much as a feather, Scintillate had already pushed back his seat and gotten to his feet, sending all the junk straight to the floor.

I stared. I'd always heard that Scintillate 'looked the part of a hero,' but it'd been ages since I actually saw him in person. At nearly seven feet in height, his shoulders were broad and his frame was well-muscled. His legs were disproportionately bulky compared to the rest of his body, which was normal for a mage of his source, though not to such an extreme as this. His hair, silver as the swords adorning his walls, was full enough to carpet the entire base. His eyes were gold with flecks of green, his teeth were white and shiny as pearls, and his skin was sunset-bronze.

"It's you," he breathed, all grumpiness instantly vanquished. He took a couple steps forward, giving off the impression of a hobnail stomping toward its prey. "I didn't know you were coming today," he laughed boisterously, like we were lifelong buddies or something—not exactly the greeting I expected after accidentally trashing his room.

But, despite his apparent cheeriness, I could immediately sense that something was off. There was a certain heaviness in his laugh—a twinge of anguish so subtle, only a hypersensitive ear-mage could've picked up on it. There was something bothering him. Something that went a lot deeper than just exhaustion from a long day. This man was seriously troubled.

I was startled by my sudden insight into Scintillate's psyche. Was I already hearing his aura in the web? Well, how could I not; it was so strong. Strong, and yet... his wavelength seemed a little too short for his color, his frequency too high. He was at the edge of the silver spectrum, almost blue. Almost as though his line were desperate to twine to someone, anyone, to sooth and slow it down.

No. I rubbed my ears. I was just hearing things. Scintillate was *surrounded* by people who adored him. For Pekoe's sake, the whole damn country was in love with him. There was no way that he could be lonely. If his photons were disordered and his aura seemed a bit off-color, it was because he was tired—something I sure as hell wasn't about to pity him for. Pekoe knew, *I* was so exhausted right now, I was about ready to pass out, right there on the stone floor.

"Auld Pharynx said you were expecting me, sir," I answered, surprised by his surprise.

"She told me I'd be getting a… helper… but she didn't say who or when."

Helper. I blinked. What an odd word choice. Wait, was the *Multi-Source Enchant* uncomfortable with the idea of having a *servant*? Didn't he grow up in a household full of them?

"The System doesn't like to tell me much of anything, if they can help it," he added, darkly.

What? Why would the government deliberately hide things from the one man on whom their hopes and dreams depended? Thank Pekoe that the System didn't make mistakes, because their decisions sure didn't make a lick of sense to me, sometimes.

"Well," I bowed, nose nearly touching the floor, "it's nice to meet you, Captain." The line, however untrue, was long overdue.

To my great surprise, Scintillate bowed back, deeply. "Nice to meet you, too. Auricle Capitulum, right?"

Yet again, I was astonished. When and where on Pekoe's island did he hear about me? At that moment, I noticed that he'd been keeping his voice down, this entire time. Besides my parents, he was the first person to do that automatically, without my asking. Even my closest friends frequently forgot to accommodate my hypersensitivity.

"Yes, sir." There was a pause. "I didn't know you were the Captain of the Water Forces," I added, stupidly. "I only found out a couple hours ago, when I got my relocation notice."

"Well, then, I guess we're in the same boat." Same boat? Was that military jargon? "I didn't know that I was the Captain of the Water Forces either, until today. I mean, I knew I'd be getting *some* sort of military assignment on my twentieth birthday, but I didn't know what or where it'd be."

Forgetting manners, I let my jaw drop. "So, this is also your first night on base?"

He nodded.

"But... it's your birthday, and Summer Solstice Day."

Why would the System choose the biggest festival of the age to force the Multi-Source Enchant from his home? They couldn't let their prophet enjoy the holiday—not to mention, his birthday—and relocate him tomorrow instead?

"It's *your* birthday, too," he pointed out.
How did he know that?

"Yeah, but, I'm me and you're... well, you're *you*."

He didn't answer. He just looked at me for a moment, exuding both confusion and concern, before stooping to clean up the mess I'd made. I immediately rushed over.

"Oh no, sir, sit down," I breathed.

Scintillate didn't sit. "Many hands make light work. I don't know about you, but I'm ready for this day to be over."

We worked in silence. I made no effort to strike up further conversation. My orders were clear: I was his servant, not his friend. I was only supposed to speak when spoken to. So far, I'd already been far too chatty.

Scintillate, who was maybe three times my size, was a lot more efficient than me. Some 'helper' I was turning out to be, already. When we were finished, he actually held out his hand to pull me up. I stood on my own, difficult as it was with my severe scoliosis, pretending not to notice his gesture.

"Tomorrow, I'll meet my fleet for the first time," he said. I stayed quiet. "We're going to have a mock-battle, at sea."

Why was he telling me this? He had no obligation to inform me of his military duties or doings. Auld made it quite clear that I had 'neither the intelligence nor the right to interfere with naval matters.' I was Scintilate's housekeeper, not his soldier.

"My Second, whom I've been told is a hand mage, will act as the commander of the 'enemy' army," Scintillate went on, "and Auld Pharynx will be our supervisor and evaluator."

Something unpleasant must've flashed across my face at the mention of Auld's name, because then Scintillate grinned and chuckled, "Not her biggest fan?"

I froze. "Um…" Was this a trap? A trick to get me to say something traitorous?

Scintillate didn't wait for me to take the bait. "Well, just because Auld can be a bother doesn't mean the System's to blame. Every dragon's nest has got at least one rotten egg, right? Besides, you're an ear mage and she's a throat mage. If you two got along, it'd be an anomaly."

I just shrugged. Of course, I hated Auld. People like her gave yellow a bad name; I was ashamed to share a color with her. But,

I wasn't about to share that thought with my new master.

Scintillate's lemon-lime eyes turned curious. "So, is it true that ear mages can hear what goes on in the spectral web?"

I shrugged, again. "Past infancy, very few of us can, sir."

"Can you?"

"Yes, sir."

"You hear everything, all the time?" he breathed.

"No, thank Pekoe. Only if something happens to my own thread. Like, if someone twines to me or has a particularly poignant thought about me. Stuff like that."

Scintillate whistled under his breath. "That's incredible."

I blinked. The Multi-Source Enchant was impressed by *my* source?

"I'm also particularly sensitive to the spectrum," he added. Of course, he was. He practically owned the whole damn web. "But, it doesn't come to me audibly. More like... I can sense it, feel it. But, only sometimes. I *definitely* can't hear the thoughts of those around me, even if we're twined—that's just crazy. You're way ahead of me there, Auricle."

"Not at all, sir," I said, wondering if it were against the code of servitude to contradict one's master, even to compliment. "You're the most powerful mage in Conflagrian history," I added, monotonously.

His enormous eyes rolled. "Sure, that's what everyone says. But, I've reached adulthood and *still* can't access both my sources."

Wait, what? My stomach disappeared. I didn't dare speak a word.

"My hair is dormant," Scintillate went on. "Don't spread that around, please. The only people who know are my instructors, the Department of Prophetic Affairs and Principal Pekoe's throne advisors. My fleet and the general public are in the dark. This is classified, got it?"

I stared. He was pulling my leg, he had to be. What made Scintillate the Multi-Source Enchant if he didn't have multi-sources? And, if this was some big military secret, then—"W-why are you telling *me*, sir?"

He gave me a weird look. "You're going to be around me all the time; there's no point in hiding things from you. You'd probably wind up figuring out the truth on your own, anyway."

"So, your hair isn't active, at all?" I breathed. He touched the abundant silvery mess on his head. "It *does* possess a few photons, but I still haven't figured out how to wield them. I've worked with all the best teachers, to no avail. The System isn't planning on declaring war until my hair 'wakes up.'" His voice dropped a couple octaves as he sourly added, "Don't hold your breath."

This was crazy. Unbelievable. Earth-shattering. Horrifying.

"In any case, I understand why the System chose you for this job," he breezed on. "They wanted someone who could keep an ear on my wavelength. You know, someone who'd have my back."

So, I wasn't picked at random. I was selected. I was chosen, for my powers. Because I possessed a desirable spectral gift. So, I wasn't useless, after all?

SPRY SCINTILLATE

Since my Circle Trial, I hardly got a moment to myself. All day, every day—weekends, holidays, birthdays—I studied and trained, under strict supervision. Accordingly, I was bending; I could feel it. Bending under everyone's high expectations, the impending war, and the obscure puzzle of the prophecy. How much longer until I'd snap?

Since my prophetic title became public knowledge, I hadn't been permitted to walk outside unaccompanied, not even in my own front yard. I was under twenty-four-hour guard. When I was nine, I once snuck out of my parents' home, clad in layers of undyed burlap, the traditional dress of the Infrareds. It was the best five minutes of my post-Circle-Trial existence. I ran briskly to prevent passerby from engaging with me, trekking to the southeast end of the Dust Path, to the more impoverished neighborhoods. Stealing curious glances at the peasants' cracked windows, I beheld living-rooms littered with broken chairs, unraveling wicker tarps, rickety shelves, three-legged tables, stained robes, crumpled parchment scraps, wooden spin-tops and torn kites. The shacks' walls were bare and composed of wood or clay—no stone, bricks, stained glass nor elaborate carvings.

Leaving the Dust Path, I wandered to the south tarot fields, Ardor Village's central farming site. Though the sun wasn't up yet, the ranges were already packed with bent backs, hard at work.

I observed the group nearest to me—five Uselesses of various colors and one Infrared, all looking around eight to ten. Supervisor nowhere in sight, the blue boy started summersaulting, to the delight of the giggling purple girl and the smiley beige boy.

"Watch this, Kidni, Peach—I'm gonna do *three* turns, this time!"

Kidni and Peach. An organ mage and a skin mage.

The blue kid gave himself a running start. Then, he leapt into the air, flipped about two and a half times… and landed on his head. I gasped, anticipating a neck-snap. But, instead, he just laughed and sprung back up, like a rubber ball. A spine mage, no doubt. For the first time, I wondered what exactly was 'useless' about spine magic. Anyone else would've been rendered paralyzed by a stunt like that.

A couple kids in the gang were actually doing their jobs, digging up taro and generating an enormous pile, until the red one decided it'd be more fun to pelt the roots at his Infrared friend. That triggered a full-on crop-fight. All the while, they squealed and laughed as though flying high on a hobnail.

Standing several feet away was a boy with bright yellow ears and a noticeably hunched back.

"Come over and help me pummel Tymp!" the Infared called to him.

"I can't get any closer to you guys until you all quit yelling," yellow-ears half-whispered.

"Wait, what did you say? I cannnnn't heeeeeaaar youuuuuu!"

The ear mage crossed his arms over his head. "Shut up, shut up, shut up!"

So playful. So joyful. These were *real* children. Free to wander without a barrage of escorts. The weight of the world didn't rest on their shoulders. They weren't condemned to a future of slaughtering Nordic technophiles.

Oh, how I wished I could join them, these peasants of the fields. In a heartbeat, I'd forfeit all the honor and glory that came with my stupid prophetic title and bend my back out here with them, just to be relieved of all my impossible expectations.

To be relieved of having to kill men before I was even one, myself.

* * *

I got in trouble for sneaking out. But, only because I turned myself in; I probably wouldn't have gotten caught otherwise. I never understood what made me do it. I never thought I was *that* righteous. I was only outside for five or so minutes when I got overcome by the irresistible desire to go confess. I was stunned by the words escaping my lips. I could've easily gotten away with the whole thing. Why did I blow my own cover?

At the very least, I hoped my punishment would be lightened because of my honesty. I should've known better. The System beat me mercilessly with whips and chains. They didn't even tie me down, as they did it. Nothing prevented me from fighting back or running away. I just... didn't want to. Because I knew I deserved what I was getting. For I disobeyed the ones who ruled the nation with perfect honor and justice.

TERMINUS LECHATELIERITE

Growing up, my comrades used to ask me a lot about it. Why are you blind in your left eye? Isn't your ability to approximate distance *all screwed up?* Will you ever make it into the fleet when you *can't even see anything?*

I *did* see just fine, thank you very much. Supposedly, I didn't have good depth-perception… but, since I was one-eyed my whole life, I hadn't a clue what 'good' depth-perception was supposed to look like. So, I got along perfectly fine.

The only question of theirs that I was never able to answer was the biggest of them all: how did it happen? Because I sure as hell wasn't born this way. I was certain of that much, not because I actually remembered ever seeing out of my left eye, but because I had a scar that stretched all the way from my pupil to the tip of my jaw. So, my blindness clearly wasn't a birth defect; I was obviously attacked by something or someone when I was very young.

When I was five, I asked Sergeant Irri if he had any inkling of what might've happened. He just shrugged, claiming that I arrived at Icicle already like this.

I had only one memory of life before the academy. I wasn't sure if it was a real memory, because I didn't think it was possible to remember being a baby. The 'memory' often came up in my nightmares. I dreamt of pain, searing pain, all the way down my face. And, two voices. A woman, screaming and crying, and a man, shouting angrily.

That was it. I must've strained my mind a thousand times, but I never recalled anything more. Never discerned a single word the man or woman said. When I was six, I opened up to Irri about my dream, hoping he'd help me identify the couple. Alarm briefly flashed across his face before he smirked and told me to quit making stuff up.

"But, I'm not, sir," I'd responded. "I've had this dream, many times. I need your help with interpreting it."

"You want me to *interpret* your dream?" he spat, brows creeping up to his hairline. "You think dreams have meaning?"

"Well, maybe, sir." I shrugged. "They do for mages."

He blinked. "You're not a mage, Terminus. *Conflagrians* have visions. *Ichthyothians* have random synaptic brain activity. We aren't connected to the spectral web. Our dreams have no correlation to reality."

"But, I've had the same exact nightmare, over and over, my whole life," I insisted. "Maybe, we *are* connected to the web, but we just aren't recognizing it."

I was benched for a week after that—no mock-battles—just for suggesting the possibility that Nordics were capable of tapping into the spectrum.

Irri may've stopped me from vocalizing my so-called 'crazy' thoughts, but that didn't mean I ever stopped thinking them. Even as I graduated into the fleet at eleven. Even as I became Captain earlier this age, at nineteen.

AURICLE CAPITULUM

This morning, the System sent me inland to fetch Scintillate's fire ration. Instead of getting sent to the back of the line with all the other Uselesses and Infrareds, I now had the right to cut to the very front and gather a generous seven-day supply.

My new job didn't provide me with a uniform, badge or any other special outward markers. I just had some nicer, newer robes. Which meant that no one could tell just by looking at me that I was the prophet's personal servant.

Unfortunately, *that* didn't occur to me when I marched right up to the System rationers, slipping directly before a seven-foot tall arm mage.

"And, where do *you* think you're going, hunchback?" he spat, whacking me upside the head with his empty torch.

The impact rang through my scalp; the echo seemed to gain intensity with every passing moment. Gasping, I dropped to my knees, eyes watering, nose stinging, eardrums throbbing.

I heard a throat clear. I struggled to peer up. One of the rationers—a woman with frizzy black locks and distinct frown lines—gave me a scathing stare, down her pointed nose.

"Can I help you?" she asked, contemptuously.

I staggered to my feet, fishing my reassignment notice from my robe. "A-a week's s-supply for Mr. Spry Scintillate, p-please." I passed her my scroll with trembling hands.

At the very sight of the System-seal-emblazoned document, her entire demeanor instantly changed. She smiled, bowed and breathed, "Right away, sir," before scurrying off to do my bidding. Minutes later, she handed me enough fire to satisfy every family on the Dust Path for a month.

I always dreamed of what it'd be like to get premier service at the Pit, amongst the nobility. But, somehow, I imagined I'd be respected for my own merit, not someone

else's. When the rationer bowed to me today, it wasn't Auricle Capitulum she was
honoring, it was the Multi-Source Enchant.
I was nothing more than his shadow.

AULD PHARYNX

I was hesitant, but Ala Pinion and Xon Follicle were adamant. Spry had to learn the truth, they said. It was time.

"He's living on base now, doing a man's work, so he needs to be treated like one, for Pekoe's sake," Xon demanded. "He's not a kid, anymore."

"Not to mention, his soldiers already know," Ala chimed. "Wouldn't it be best for him to hear it straight from us?"

I rubbed my temples.

"And, what if the Nordics strike on Conflagrian soil, at some point?" Xon added. "He needs to be made aware of the importance of protecting what's in the Fire Pit, at all costs."

I nodded. "You're both right, of course. I know that. I've just been dreading this day since the boy was born."

"We're in for a rough seven minutes," Ala agreed. "But, it'll pass quickly enough and things will go right back to normal; you'll see."

A thought suddenly occurred to Xon: "What about Auricle?"

I blinked. "What about him?"

"Do we tell him, too?"

There was a pause.

"I suppose." Ala shrugged. "If we don't, Spry will. He shares *everything* with his servant. Pekoe only knows why."

I nodded. "What could Auricle possibly do, anyway? He's no threat to anybody."

* * *

We decided to tell them at the same time. Auricle sat quietly and didn't ask questions. But, Spry, on the other hand—

"Spectral *direction?*" he breathed, golden-green eyes growing wider by the second. "What you're describing sounds more like *suppression.*"

"It's for their own good," Xon said. "Without it, there'd be chaos, civil war, rebellion..."

Spry stood, towering over us. "Yeah, because you'd be giving them something to rebel against!"

I checked my spectral sundial. Four minutes left.

"Spry, please, open your eyes," Xon pleaded, "look around you. Everybody is content. Happy. You live in a utopia. Conflagria's never experienced a *single* domestic dispute. Not one, in seven eras. Do you realize how incredible that is? No crime, no violence, no discontentment. What is freedom but the privilege to live in perfect peace?"

"If our peace is so perfect, why the hell are we getting ready to go to war with Ichthyosis?"

"That's an entirely different—"

"You know what freedom is?" he growled, fists balled. "Freedom is the right to *choose* between right and wrong. To *decide* if you're content or not."

"How would the choice to be disgruntled and unruly help anyone?"

"It'd help by making us human beings, not penned-up scabrouses!"

Two more minutes.

"Spry, sometimes, it's necessary to make personal sacrifices for the greater good—"

"Who are *you* to decide what sacrifices must be made by every man, woman and child on the island?"

"Who are we?" Xon roared. "We're the System!"

Spry exhaled through his nostrils. "Well, then, maybe, you shouldn't be. Maybe, someone else should run this damn country. Someone who'd actually care to *learn* right from wrong before thrusting their own corrupt definitions into the minds of generations!"

At this point, Auricle was cowering under Spry's desk, hood drawn and arms crossed over his head.

One minute.

"Am I affected by it, too?" Spry asked, hands trembling.

"Yes," Xon replied.

Spry's lids closed. "How much time have I got left?"

Xon exhaled. "You're down to your last seconds."

Spry began to pace about the room, faster and faster. At last, with a loud grunt, he kicked his bed, which was no small matter for a leg mage of his caliber. The whole structure—mattress, frame, headboard and all—literally flew up to the ceiling before crashing down with near-seismic force. Auricle wailed.

"Get out," Spry boomed, advancing on us. "All of you, get out, right now, before I kill you!"

Without another word, Ala, Xon and I obeyed. I peered at my wrist.

Spry should've succumbed over a minute ago.

AURICLE CAPITULUM

Auld, Ala and Xon couldn't leave fast enough for Scintillate. He slammed the door after them with a mighty bang. I whimpered.

Scintillate didn't seem to notice me. I stayed under his desk, bent back accommodating the tight space. And, I watched in horror as the Great Prophet of Conflagria collapsed face-down onto his bed and sobbed at the top of his lungs, like a terrified child.

If seven minutes was indeed the limit, Scintillate should've succumbed already. He was on his way, I could tell: just seconds ago, he had the energy for rage and violence, whereas now, he only had the strength to weep.

I also got a bit angry, but just for a brief moment after the System admins broke the news. Even then, I was distracted by the swell of painful noises filling the room. Currently, all I felt was anxiety over what to do next. My job was to serve Scintillate, to assist him with whatever he needed. He clearly needed help, right now. But, I hadn't the slightest idea what'd be appropriate to provide. I knew what action a *friend* would take at a time like this, but what did a *servant* do when his master cried and wailed? Fetch him a pail of water?

Well, I was certain that I was supposed to do *something* besides crouching here indefinitely, like a coward.

I crawled out, brazenly sat beside Scintillate on his bed, held out my handkerchief and awkwardly said, "Um, sorry 'bout all this, sir."

To my profound dismay, my words just made Scintillate bawl harder. He sat up, tears dotting his silver lashes and bronze face. He took my rag and blew his nose in it with a powerful rumble.

"It's sick," he choked, "it's twisted. I can't be their prophet anymore, Auricle, I just can't do it." He hiccupped. "How can I serve a master whose cause I don't believe in, anymore?"

Serve a master? I froze. Did Spry really see himself as a... a *servant?*

"You'll be able to return to duty, sooner or later," was all I said, calmly and quietly. "The Crystal won't let you feel this way for much longer."

AULD PHARYNX

Spry stayed in bed for three full days. While he didn't have the strength for an ongoing violent opposition, his dominion over the spectral web enabled him to pull off a seventy-two-hour sleeping-strike.

On the fourth day, Spry returned to duty without a peep about the Core Crystal. But, it was obvious he was still thinking about it, every minute. He no longer laughed nor bantered with his comrades. He wasn't quite as quick to offer creative solutions to the hypothetical battle-scenarios we presented to him in practice. His wild flare was gone. His every word and movement was listless, lifeless.

We damaged our own Water Forces Captain. By telling him the truth, we broke him. Now, the real question was what to do with the pieces. Because, there was no way we could declare war on Ichthyosis as long as our top military leader remained so disillusioned.

It was obvious to Xon, Ala and I that the boy's anger—whether expressed as lethargy or rage—was here to stay, in some capacity. There was no going back to the pre-revelation, happy-go-lucky Spry we all knew. So, we figured, the best thing to do now was help divert his hatred from us, focusing it where it belonged.

Every day, he and his men attended 'Enemy Life and Culture' class, in which his teachers regularly emphasized Nordickind's responsibility for Conflagria's obscurity in the international arena. Spry listened, took notes, asked questions, scored well on quizzes. He was clearly absorbing everything that was disseminated, at least on an intellectual level. But, we had no idea what was actually going on in his heart. We needed him to really internalize the rhetoric, developing a strong 'us-versus-them' mentality. We wanted him to develop a powerful thirst for vengeance.

By the end of the week, we decided to put Spry's loyalties to the test, as our spectrometers indicated that he was finally succumbing to the Crystal *just* enough to be incapable of lying to System staff.

On the eve of our confrontation, Xon and Ala came to my office to discuss exactly how we'd broach the topic with Spry.

"I just think, 'do you hate the Nordics?' is a bit too... I don't know, heavy-handed," I argued. "The word 'hate' may put his guard up. We already pushed him too hard, once. Caution is needed, now more than ever."

"I don't see what's so unreasonable about asking our *Water Forces Captain* to hate his *enemy*," Ala shot. "We're about to send the boy to war, for Pekoe's sake. If he's lukewarm on this, there's no telling what kind of decisions he'll make in combat."

Xon nodded. "Yes, *disliking* isn't enough. Only *hate* entails dehumanization: he can't think of the Nordics as people, if he has to kill them. Knowing Spry, that'd tear him apart."

That much was true. Some people were born killers, able to depreciate human life when the time called, without a second thought. Spry wasn't one of them, not by a longshot. He believed that every life was precious. It was his greatest weakness.

"Fine," I snorted. "Ask him point-blank. Just don't get your hopes up."

There was a tense silence.

"Auld, this is something we need to know, beyond a shadow of a doubt," Ala insisted. "The line between hate and dislike could mean the difference between victory and defeat. We must find out *exactly* where Spry falls on that spectrum, no ambiguity. But, that doesn't mean we have to shove words in his mouth. When we talk to him tomorrow evening, let's just gently ask him how his Nordic Studies class is going, encouraging him to express his feelings on his own."

Xon nodded. "And, then, the following morning, we'll give him some material to help nudge him along—like, the scroll the intelligence agency has been putting together." He stroked his goatee. "Learning about the nebulous 'Nordic race' isn't enough, anymore; it's time we put a name and face to his greatest opponent, so he knows exactly to whom his utmost hatred is due: Diving Fleet Captain Terminus Expiri Lechatelierite."

"But, let's not be the ones to hand him the scroll ourselves," Ala spouted. "Let's give it to Auricle, to pass along. Spry takes things better when they come from Auricle."

"Yes, he does. For Pekoe's sake, you'd think they were *friends* or something," I grunted. "I don't understand how someone of Spry's mental caliber could possibly find such a relationship satisfying, in any capacity."

Xon shrugged. And, with that, he and Ala got to their feet, bowed and left.

I exhaled, a strange sensation pricking my chest. I knew what it was. Fear.

"Xon," I called, when he was halfway down the corridor. He scurried back.

"Ma'am?"

"Xon, what'll happen if Spry doesn't pull through, in the end?"

Xon understood what I meant. Not the end of tomorrow. But, the *real* end. The war.

Fireplace flames danced in his oil-black eyes. He stood as still as a stone gargoyle.

"We'll wait," he murmured. "Just, wait." He didn't say for what.

AURICLE CAPITULUM

I was so nervous, I could literally hear the *thump-swish, thump-swish* of blood pumping through my veins. I stood, transfixed in the corridors outside Auld's office, effortlessly eavesdropping on her conversation with Ala and Xon. I didn't set out to spy, tonight—I stumbled upon their chat accidentally, on my way back from the outhouse—but, I was still wrought with guilt, nonetheless. I knew I only had seven minutes before the Crystal would compel me to plug my ears and flee the scene. Seven, if I was lucky. Honestly, I doubted I'd last five.

"I don't see what's so unreasonable about asking our *Water Forces Captain* to hate his *enemy,*" Ala's voice rang. "We're about to send the boy to war, for Pekoe's sake. If he's lukewarm on this, there's no telling what kind of decisions he'll make in combat."

"Yes, *disliking* isn't enough," Xon chimed. "Only *hate* entails dehumanization: he can't think of the Nordics as people, if he has to kill them. Knowing Spry, that'd tear him apart."

"Fine," Auld spat. "Ask him point-blank. Just don't get your hopes up."

Already, my mind was struggling to re-member the words I just heard. The Crystal was fighting to derail my focus.

"Learning about the nebulous 'Nordic race' isn't enough, anymore," Xon was saying. "It's time we put a name and face to his greatest opponent, so he knows exactly to whom his utmost hatred is due: Diving Fleet Captain Terminus Expiri Lechatelierite."

I blinked. The System didn't make mis-takes, everyone knew that. But, I must've been missing something here, because it sure seemed to me like they were about to make a rather big one. *People* had faces. Not enemies. If Spry believed that every life was precious, how would *humanizing* his opponent help motivate him toward hatred and violence!?

"But, let's not be the ones to hand him the scroll ourselves," Ala said. "Let's give it to Auricle, to pass along. Spry takes things better when they come from Auricle."

At this, I'd reached my breaking point. Palms to my ears, I sprinted full-speed down the hall.

* * *

The moment the wakeup chimes sounded, Auld called me to her office to hand me the infamous document, bound up with a big red bow like a Summer Solstice Day present.

"Give this to your master after our talk with him tonight," was all she said. "Dismissed."

I bowed and stepped out, closing the door behind me.

Feeling the painful pangs of defiance, I untied the ribbon and unrolled the scroll.

"Ter-min-us Luh-shhhaht-leeeer-aahyyyt," I slowly sounded-out the Ichthyothian Captain's complicated name, under my breath. For Pekoe's sake, did all Nordic names sound like clay pots banging and scraping together, or just his?

My eyes slid down the parchment, halting at the striking image of the man's paper-white face and chilling blue eyes. His cheeks were sucked in, like that of the poorest peasants, and he had a grotesque slash running all the way from his left eye to the edge of his sharp jaw. Transfixed and horrified, I stroked my own stubbly cheek. Did someone try to slice his head open, or what?

I rolled the thing back up with trembling hands. I knew giving this info to Spry was a bad idea. It wouldn't help the System accomplish what they wanted—on the contrary. But, I had no choice but to do as I was told. It wasn't my place to question the manner in which the System handled Spry. My job was to make Spry's bed and fetch him water and wash his smelly uniforms. Not analyze his psyche and modify the System's training methods accordingly. Never mind that I spent hours upon hours with him every day and probably already knew him far better than anybody. Never mind that I actually cared to listen to him when no one else did. Never mind that I was the only mage on earth to have ever been inside Spry's own head, thinking his thoughts and dreaming his dreams.

AULD PHARYNX

Class and practice were through for the day; Xon, Ala and I now followed Spry to his room and stood before his desk. Slouching in his seat, Spry looked up at us with impassive eyes, though clearly aware that something serious was about to go down. Auricle was already rolling up tiny shreds of parchment and shoving them into his ears.

"Spry," Xon began, voice calm and—a bit overly—casual, "we were just wondering," his hand flew up to his goatee, "how have things been going for you, in Nordic Studies class?"

Pekoe, was that vague. I knew we wanted to be careful and all, refraining from putting words in the boy's mouth, but this was maybe a little *too* hands-off.

Silence.

"What's it been like for you," Ala awkwardly chimed, "learning about the Ichthyothians?"

I fought the urge to cringe openly. Ugh, non-throat mages had terrible vocal control. I should've been the one to break the ice, tonight.

Spry blinked. "What's it *been like?*"

"Yes."

He thought for a while, honey-moss gaze floating in the empty space above our heads.

"Well, their technology presents a formidable obstacle for us, though not insurmountable," he answered, monotonously. "In some ways, it gives them a distinct edge. For example, their seacrafts—particularly the small arrow-like submarines they call 'crystallines'—are faster and more maneuverable than our own dragon ships and quartz fighters. Yet, their tech could also be construed as a handicap, as their entire society is completely reliant on external gadgets not only for combat, but for mere survival. To an extent, Nordics know how to manipulate the electromagnetic spectrum to their ends—they have x-ray machines for medical diagnoses, for example—but, they have no organic, biological ability to do so, and more importantly, they consider our powers to be 'supernatural'—in other words, something that cannot be understood from a logical or scientific perspective. I believe that this ignorance could be the key to our victory in the forthcoming war. If they were to truly comprehend the technical discipline of spectroscopy and the methodic manner in which our kind operates the 'magical' web to our advantage, we'd risk losing that advantage."

Xon and Ala were visibly uncomfortable. Spry's analysis was clear, concise and spot-on. The problem was, it was an *analysis*. For once, we didn't want an academic or intellectual response. We wanted emotion. We wanted to know how Spry *felt* about the Nordics, not what he'd learned about them in class.

Xon smiled. "Excellent synthesis of your coursework," he commended. "But, I didn't mean to be testing your comprehension of the material presented in lecture. We know you understand that quite well; your test scores are proof enough. I was asking your *opinion* on the Nordics."

"My... opinion?" Spry breathed, as though the very concept of having one was outrageous.

"Yes."

Spry blinked again. "Well... um... I guess I haven't really thought about that."

"Is that so?" I interjected. Maybe, Spry *was* able to lie to us, after all.

His temples pulsed. "I mean, it's *obvious* what the teachers are trying to get us to think. I just don't know if I'm there, yet."

My stomach jumped a couple inches up my esophagus. "How do you mean?"

He shrugged. "The Ichthyothians haven't done anything to me, yet. Why should I hate them?"

My foot tapped. "Well, Spry, because they've actually already done plenty. They're responsible for our nation's expulsion from the Second Earth Order."

"Yeah, but wasn't that, like, four eras ago?"

"It doesn't matter if it were forty eras ago. Conflagria is still suffering the consequences until today."

Spry's enormous glassy eyes rolled. "The Nordics who made the decision to blacklist Conflagria are long dead. I'm not going to hold a grudge against the current generation for what their ancestors did, four hundred ages ago."

"But, they haven't changed their minds about us, even after all this time. Not only are they actively upholding their ancestors' political ruling, their culture breeds deep prejudices against all things magical."

"And, you think that trying to steal their land and slaughter their men will change their minds about us?" Spry snorted, getting riled up already. Auricle dropped to his hands and knees, ready to escape beneath the furniture, again. "What they did back then was wrong, yes, but we sure aren't making it right now by picking a fight. If the Nordics believe that we're violent savages, and we want to prove we're not, why are we going over there with weapons and soldiers instead of diplomats and ambassadors?"

"Ambassadors? Wake up, Spry!" Xon roared, and Auricle whimpered. "Do you think the Ichthyothians would be *willing* to host a mage ambassador?"

"I don't know; why don't we *ask* them?"

Auricle lay on his stomach beneath Spry's bed, hood drawn and arms crossed over his head.

I supposed we had our answer.

AURICLE CAPITULUM

After about twenty more minutes of futile argument, the System admins finally left. I breathed a sigh of relief as the door closed behind them.

I crawled out from under Spry's bed, overcome by a sense of déjà-vu. It was the debacle of last week, all over again! Except, this time, Spry didn't have the energy to cry or kick things. He just stared blankly at the floor, cheeks in his palms.

I wondered what would become of him. I was irritated at Auld, Ala and Xon for messing with his head again, so soon. Maybe, the dragon dung wouldn't have hit the fan so hard if they'd given him another week or so, to fall further under the Crystal's spell. If only they knew him as well as I did—if only they took the time to actually *listen* to him, like me—they wouldn't have underestimated his capacity to resist.

I felt sorry for Spry, the very man I grew up envying and loathing. Day after day, it was becoming all the more apparent to me that bearing the prophetic title wasn't what it was cracked up to be. It wasn't all glory and honor and luxury. It was insane hours of work and study and training; it was knowing that the whole country was watching your every move and expecting nothing less from you than inhuman perfection. It was living with an aura *just* strong enough to teeter the line between independence and submission, rather than comfortably resting on either side.

It was weird to think that I now actually sympathized with someone like Spry; I never thought I'd see the day. While we came from completely different classes and backgrounds, our struggles were parallel, in many ways. Neither of us had any control over our lives. Both of us were overworked pawns of society. Both of us had to fight for our reputations: Spry, to live up to the hype, and me, to prove that I wasn't as worthless as my Circle Trial indicated.

Spry's personality didn't fit the stereotypical mold of nobility. He was neither cocky nor entitled nor insolent. He saw the prophecy as a serious responsibility, not a means to boast nor mistreat. He never used his spectral prowess or social prominence for personal gain. His concern was wholly for us, for Conflagria. He thought of himself as a servant, a protector. Not a hero.

Late last night, I heard a few thoughts of his, through the spectral web. They didn't come to me as clear sentences. More like, hunches and feelings. My initial reaction was to deny them, because they wracked me with guilt; Spry didn't know just how bitter I'd been toward him, my whole life—how my friends and I used to curse his name and throw rotten scabrous eggs at his palace.

Surprisingly, Spry thought of me as a friend. He was even arranging with a hand-mage comrade to get me some chiropractic therapy. I couldn't understand why he'd give a dragon turd about me. It wasn't like I was particularly kind to him. I just did my duty. And, not well, either. I asked too many questions, frequently got lost in the corridors while running errands and, thanks to my advancing scoliosis, couldn't lift very much. Not to mention, continually accommodating my hypersensitive ear magic must've been annoying as hell.

I was even more shocked to learn that Spry often wished he were in my place. Since he snuck out of his parents' home at age ten and saw me and my friends in the fields, he frequently dreamed of leaving nobility behind. Even before he learned about the Core Crystal. That was just the grain of sand that broke the scabrous's back.

He sat before me now, head in his hands, winded and upset. Inside the pocket of my robe, my fingers traced the wrinkled edges of the scroll that bore the biography of the Ichthyothian Sea Captain—the scroll I knew would only make things worse.

"What's going to happen to me, Auricle?" Spry murmured to his sandals. "I can't fight their war. Not like this. Every time I think about the Crystal and what they've done with it, I lose the will to serve their cause."

"Then, stop thinking about it," I blandly voiced. "I hate to say this, sir, but you're just going to have to quit resisting. What other option do you have? You're bound to submit in the end, anyway—the Crystal won't let you struggle with this forever." At least, I hoped not. "So, there's no point in torturing yourself along the way, right? You might as well save yourself—and everybody else—a lot of grief by cooperating."

It was a nervy thing for anyone, let alone a lowly servant, to suggest to the Multi-Source Enchant. But, apparently, to Spry, I wasn't just anyone. And, to me, he wasn't just the Multi-Source Enchant. I had no choice but to admit it to myself, now: we were friends. And, friends were supposed to want the best for one another. Friends said what *needed* to be said, no matter how harsh.

Spry didn't answer. I figured that he didn't have the energy to argue anymore, not even with me. He just curled up into a ball and went to sleep, not bothering to change out of his uniform or crawl under his blanket.

The next morning, I could tell that he was actually trying to take my words to heart, because he returned to duty without a word.

AURICLE CAPITULUM

I gave Spry the scroll after his pre-breakfast swim.

"What's that?" he asked as I retrieved it from my robe pocket. He gestured for me to place it on his desk so he could finish toweling his sopping hair. In an official capacity, I had no idea how Spry was doing in his dormant-source training, but the manual drying was definitely a bad sign, as hair mages were supposed to possess the ability to spontaneously and instantly eradicate all moisture from their locks.

"Well, um…" I hesitated.

"They didn't tell you?" Spry slung the soggy towel over his shoulder, snatched up the parchment and started yanking off the ribbon I'd sloppily retied. "Typical System." His eyes rolled. "I told them not to bother hiding stuff from you, since I always share everything with you anyway, but they just keep on being paranoid sons of b—" His voice went dead as his eyes raced down the bio. "Oh, Pekoe," he breathed.

"Yeah, that Luhssshhhahtleerahyt guy is pretty creepy, isn't he, sir?" I babbled. "As spindly as a premature scabrous." As if *that* were the most striking aspect of his appearance.

"Forget that, what I want to know is how he got that nasty scar." Spry touched his own cheek.

I didn't like what I saw now in Spry's golden-green gaze: sympathy. Thirty seconds with the scroll, and the man was already having warm-fuzzies for his arch-nemesis.

"Yeah, I wonder what he did, to get cut like that," I murmured.

Lechatelierite's picture had triggered an entirely different response in me. My reaction was revulsion and fear, not compassion. I thought the scar made him look feral, evil and downright freaky.

"Or rather, what someone *else* did." Spry looked up at me. "The war hasn't even started yet, and the man's already been wounded."

"You're not supposed to feel sorry for him," I retorted, a bit disgusted. "In battle, he'd kill you in a hot second, you know."

"I bet the Childhood Program is responsible for it," Spry went on, eyes narrowed to citrus slits. "It's so uncivilized, what they're doing to those kids. I wish there was some way I could put a stop to it."

For Pekoe's sake! "Oh, so, now, you want to reform the Nordic military to make life better for your enemies?" My hands waved. "Earth to Captain Scintillate! You're in the *System* Water Forces."

Spry ignored me. "Terminus Expiri Lechatelierite," he read the man's foreign name far more fluently than I. Though, his swift pronunciation still didn't prevent it from sounding like a stack of clay plates shattering on the floor. Ichthyothian was such a violent and consonant tongue, full of harsh articulations and hacking and spitting. Everything sounded like bickering.

"Such an ugly name, isn't it, sir?" I now asked Spry.

"Not if you know what it means. End Crystal. Crystal's End. I think it's poetic.

Though, it kind of sounds like a bad omen, if you ask me…" He regarded me, thoughtfully. "Have you ever seen a lechatelierite?" he asked, suddenly. "The crystal, I mean."

"It's a type of crystal?"

He nodded. "Typically, lechatelierites are byproducts of lightning strikes in sand, meteor impacts or, in some recorded First-Earth cases, nuclear explosions. Such a fascinating history."

Thunderstorms, meteors and bombs. "Such a *violent* history, you mean."

At the mention of violence, Spry went silent.

SPRY SCINTILLATE

I couldn't bring myself to hate him.

I knew that was what the System wanted from me, but I just couldn't force my heart to take that leap. I was captivated by his life-story—how he was taken at birth from his parents because they couldn't afford to pay the firstborn-son-draft exemption fee, was raised on a military base and would've sped through the grade-levels and ranks even faster than he did, if it weren't for his 'crazy' childhood interest in spectroscopy.

Ironically, the attribute that made Lechat-elierite a particularly-dangerous threat to magekind was the very trait that the Trilateral Committee considered to be his greatest flaw. The biggest advantage we magic-folk had over the Nordics was our ability to manipulate the optical range of the electromagnetic spectrum. As long as the Ichthyothians believed our 'magic' was 'supernatural'—exempt from the rational, empirical laws of science—they wouldn't figure out how to use it against us. Because, auras or no auras, they probably *could* negatively impact the spectral web if they tried; after all, they had spectroscopes, spectrometers, Doppler radars, electromagnetic inductors and transistors.

Their ignorance was crucial to our survival. But, a curious and brilliant mind like Lechatelierite's threatened that ignorance. I could only hope that the Trilateral Committee had put an end to his dabbling in the field, by now. The last thing we needed to face in combat was a frightening fusion of technology and magic.

But, despite the danger Lechatelierite posed, and despite the System's urgent promptings, I couldn't bring myself to loath the young Captain. How could I hate him when he was a foot-soldier just like me, controlled by overlords with their own agendas, forced to fight their wars? The Trilateral Committee dictated Lechatelierite's every breath since his birth, not unlike the System did with me. We were both considered the hopes of our peoples. We both had no choice but to submit to our superiors' plots. I couldn't resist—at least, not effectively—because of the Core Crystal. Lechatelierite couldn't because he'd been actively brainwashed for nearly two decades, not to mention that his country was in imminent danger of being taken over. By me.

I studied his smooth, childlike face. It was hard to believe that he was born in the eighty-seventh age, only six months after me. His height and weight stats were what I'd expect from a boy of twelve, not nineteen.

His right eye was astute and sea-blue. His left was half-closed, lid and pupil bisected. Apparently, according to the scroll, it wasn't a battle-scar. Not really. He'd sustained it in infancy, before he ever set foot on a military base. Yet, the war was still the reason for it.

His parents were unable to afford the firstborn-son-draft exemption fee. They were desperate to dodge it. So desperate, in fact, that they were willing to hurt their own baby to disqualify him. They figured that whatever harm they inflicted couldn't possibly be worse than what he'd face if sent off to war. Prosthetic limb technology was too good in Ichthyosis; they knew that merely amputating an arm or leg wouldn't be serious enough to make the Trilateral Committee dismiss him. So, they searched for something else, a different injury to inflict. Something irreversible. Visual reparation bands were powerful, but they couldn't reverse total blindness. So, with Terminus's father holding him down, his mother got to work with a kitchen knife. But, halfway through the 'procedure,' she panicked and screwed up, slashing his cheek.

After that, the government had no choice but to remove Terminus from his home anyway; his parents were convicted of child-abuse and incarcerated.

The story made me want to vomit. The fact that a mother and father could do such a thing to their own child—no matter the intention—made me sick inside. I wondered if Terminus knew the reason for his handicap. If not, I wondered what excuses Icicle gave the boy, if any.

I was astonished that the Nordics were willing to put a half-blind, dragon-turd-sized kid at the head of their elite Diving Fleet. He must've had one hell of a brilliant mind, to compensate for his serious physical shortcomings. Here in Conflagria, physical prowess was everything. It determined your worth in society. I was made Captain of the Water Forces not because I was particularly bright nor talented, but because I was a big, bulky guy with a high Blood-Spectrum Content. Auricle was both clever and kind, yet society considered him trash because his magic was impractical and he had a crooked spine. If someone like Lechatelierite lived *here,* he'd be ridiculed and cast aside, not esteemed and elevated.

Then again, if Lechatelierite were born here, he'd still have two fully-functional eyes.

I tucked the scroll in my desk drawer. Time for dormant-source training. I jogged down the corridors, trying to force Lechatelierite's scarred face from my mind.

But, all day long, that milky-blue eye followed me.

SPRY SCINTILLATE

The end of the day couldn't come quickly enough. Exhausted and demotivated from yet another fruitless adventure in hair-mage training, I was ready to burrow under the covers and conk out.

Auricle always hid behind a screen when he changed. I supposed he was embarrassed by his bent back and thin limbs.

"I was just wondering, sir," he said as he stepped out, fully clothed, "are sources hereditary?"

It was a good question. I knew that color wasn't necessarily; my mother's aura was blue and my father's was green.

"I don't know." I studied his worried face. "I guess I've never really thought about it, before."

He smirked. "Of course, *you* wouldn't have. Your bloodline's got nothing to worry about, for at least three or four generations."

I shrugged. "Life has a way of playing tricks on us. I wouldn't be surprised if a Useless cropped up among my future kids or grandkids."

Auricle's eyes rolled. "Uh huh, sure." He gave me a lopsided grin. "That'll happen the day the System starts writing off multi-sourced mages."

"With their track-record," I murmured, curling beneath my blanket, "you never know."

* * *

It began with alcohol wipes and ice packs. I stood, transfixed and horrified, in the corner of the young couple's kitchen.

"Stop!" I yelled, but they carried on as if I were mute and invisible. "Don't do it; they're going to take him, no matter what! This isn't going to save him!"

Gurgling obliviously, the baby's enormous sea-blue eyes looked up at the glinting knife. The blade descended. Screaming, I threw myself before it and—

The kitchen abruptly vanished from around me; instead, I found myself standing in the middle of a dusty taro field, hot wind whipping my robe and hair into a frenzy.

What on Pekoe's island? How did I get here? Where did the Lechatelierite family go?

A thin blonde boy in a faded yellow robe walked right past me, an immense burlap sack over his shoulder. He moaned as he hoisted it onto a wagon bed, alongside dozens of others.

Could it be? "Auricle!" I ran to him, kicking up clouds of sand. "Auricle, you've got to help me! I just came from Ichthyosis and saw Lechatelierite's parents about to blind him—we've got to find a way back, right now, and—"

My voice died in my throat as Auricle turned and stalked away. He squatted by another bag, almost twice the size as the last. He heaved and heaved, to no avail. A whine issued from his lips.

"Auricle?" I approached him slowly. He was a lot shorter than I remembered. And, his back was less bent. I perused his face. Smooth. Unblemished.

Of course. I'd made another jump through time. *This* Auricle was what, now, twelve? Thirteen? So, it was too late to save Terminus. Sorrow and helplessness pricked my chest.

Auricle went right on, yanking and tugging and panting and grunting, but no matter what, the satchel wouldn't budge.

"Stop," I told him, "please. Can't you see it's much too heavy for you? You're only going to injure yourself, if you keep at it." I stepped forward. "Here, let me get it for you."

But, my hand passed right through it, as though I were a ghost.

At last, Auricle gave up. He collapsed onto the ground, face red and chest heaving.

"Useless!" snapped a sharp voice from behind. I swiveled around and saw a field supervisor marching in our direction, arms folded and magical throat glowing. "What are you doing? On your feet!"

Auricle jumped. "I'm s-sorry, Mr. Vo-chord, sir," he whispered.

"If I catch you slacking again, I'm revoking your food and fire for another week!" Vochord thundered. *Another* week? "Get your lazy ass back in line!"

"Not so loud," I scolded the throat mage. "He's an ear mage; can't you tell you're hurting him?"

"I-I wasn't slacking, sir," Auricle sputtered. "I swear—"

"Silence! Back to work, NOW!"

Whimpering, Auricle clamped his hands over his ears.

So, Vochord advanced on him, forcibly grabbing his wrists and shouting, "How DARE you ignore me like that, you WORTHLESS heap of dragon dung!"

"I-I'm not, sir, I-I swear." Auricle cried, tearfully. "It's j-just that my hearing is very—"

Throwing Auricle to the sand, Vochord kicked him viciously in the face, back, gut, chest—

"No!" I cried. "Stop! For Pekoe's sake, he's only a child!"

Something shook my shoulder. I opened my eyes—a strange thing to do, when I thought they were already open.

Auricle was standing over me. Twenty-age-old Auricle.

"You," I breathed stupidly, sitting up in bed, sheets tangled around my body.

"Sir?" He gave me a strange look. "You were calling out in your sleep."

I said nothing. I just stared unblinkingly back, unable—or, unwilling—to believe that he was the same mage as the little boy I just saw writhing in the sand, howling in agony.

"Are you alright?" he asked.

Was *I* alright? The real question was, was *he* alright?

"Yeah, I'm... fine."

"Are you sure?"

I studied his spine. More than twice as bent now than in my vision.

"Never mind me," I breathed, wiping my sweaty face in my blanket. "I've been meaning to tell you that I'm arranging some chiropractic therapy for your back. One of my comrades is a hand mage who used to be a medicine man."

Auricle cocked his head, surprised by the sudden topic change. "Sir?" he chirped, again.

"I'll get him to work on you, first thing in the morning," I went on. "And, then, you can have the rest of the day off."

Auricle's jaw literally unhinged. "The day off?" he gasped. "What for?"

I shrugged. "You haven't had one since we got here."

He blinked. "We haven't been here for very long, sir. Maybe, ten days?"

"And, please don't call me 'sir,' anymore. It's weird when people my same age do that. I'm Spry, okay?"

"O-okay, sir." Auricle paused, then laughed. "Woops! Sorry, si—Spry!"

I grinned. "It's fine. Old habits die hard."

As did old mindsets. But, it was about time that I quit feeling sorry for myself every day, wishing that I could escape my burdens in the taro fields. Apparently, peasant life wasn't as carefree as I'd assumed. They had vicious wars of their own. Wars I was totally ignorant of, until now.

Auricle was poor, uneducated and systematically abused because of his impractical source. Terminus was handicapped, isolated and brainwashed because his parents couldn't afford to buy his freedom. But, I had powerful magic, wealth, honor and a family who wouldn't dare dream of plucking a spectrally-dormant hair from my head. And, I had the audacity to pity myself?

TERMINUS LECHATELIERITE

She pulled open the utensil drawer, searching for the sharpest knife. Her hands trembled already, as she wiped it with rubbing alcohol.

"We're saving his life," a male voice reassured her. "If they send him to war, he won't make it. Not with his condition."

"Why isn't his mild proportionate-dwarfism enough of a reason to disqualify him, in the first place?" the woman whimpered, sweaty reflection peering anxiously from the gleaming blade.

"I don't know," the man quietly answered. "But, since it isn't, they've left us no choice."

She nodded somberly and moved toward the counter, where the baby lay. The man held an ice-pack over the child's left eye for several minutes before tossing it noisily into the sink. He held the boy down as she leaned in. Finally, the silver tip met the infant's pink lid. The boy opened his tiny mouth, emitting a bloodcurdling howl that filled the whole kitchen.

His cries were soon accompanied by the woman's screams and the man's curses. Panicking, the woman jolted, blade sliding all the way to the child's chin. Rivers of scarlet flooded his flushed face—

I sat up in bed, shivering and sobbing and pawing my numb left cheek. That was it. That was how my scar came to be. Though I didn't have a colored electromagnetic field, I was positive that what I just saw was real. It was a vision. A flashback. A glimpse into my past, delivered to my lifeline via the spectral web.

And, for the first time in many ages, tears escaped the corner of my right eye.

AURICLE CAPITULUM

No work for twenty-four consecutive hours. The very concept was as alien to me as a snowstorm. I couldn't remember the last time I had an entire day to myself.

But, before I could take a wagon inland, Auld summoned me to her office, flanked by both Ala and Xon. Great.

I bowed deeply, nerves jangling. "Sirs, ma'am."

Auld gave me a sour-scabrous-milk smile, gesturing to the chair across from her desk. "Please, sit down."

Please? The polite word sounded so foreign, issuing from her lips. Something smelled fishy.

"We just wanted to ask you how the Captain's been?" Xon inquired, oh-so-casually.

I blinked. What an odd thing *not* to ask Spry directly. "He doesn't tell you himself, sir?"

Xon chuckled. "People don't always volunteer what's truly on their minds. It often
takes another to see what's really going on,
deep down."

"Deep down?" I stared, blankly. "I make
his bed and fold his laundry."

Xon stroked his goatee, amusement and
impatience warring with one another, on
his rugged face. "You two don't talk?"

I shrugged. "Sometimes. Small talk, mostly.
He's usually too busy or tired for much else."

Apparently, Auld had already grown tired
of waiting for me to decipher Xon's cryptic
inquires, because then she abruptly jumped
at me with: "How has he been responding to
the scroll on the Ichthyothian Sea Captain?"

So, *that's* what this was all about. Of
course. They didn't want to poke the sleep-
ing dragon again so soon, so instead they
came to his harmless servant for info.

"He... hasn't said much, ma'am," I lied,
and immediately, my heart began to race. It
was my second act of direct defiance, this
week alone. Did I have the stamina to take
on the Crystal back-to-black, like this?

Xon's fingers twirled the beard-curl at the
tip of his butt-like chin. "Nothing, at all?

No snide remarks about the Nordic boy's
blindness or dwarfism or funny-sounding
name? No inkling of excitement to face him
off in battle?"

I wondered if they knew Spry at all, to
think he'd react that way. Snide remarks?
Ridicule? Excitement? Did they think Spry
was a calloused monster, to look forward to
killing? Didn't they study First-Earth history and learn that, in war—no matter the
outcome—the soldier never wins?

"No, sir." It felt good to answer a question
truthfully. It eased a little bit of the pain.

"Well, what about his thoughts?" Auld
bellowed—much too loudly, of course.
"Hear anything of significance through the
spectral web, lately?"

My stomach creeped up my esophagus.
Oh, yes, I certainly did. He had quite a
nightmare, last night.

"With all due respect, ma'am, his thoughts
are his own," I found my lips saying. Instantly, sweat droplets began to break out
on my forehead.

Auld gave a phony high-pitched laugh
that made my eardrums rattle. "I understand
your desire to protect your master; it's only

natural. But, there's no need to guard him from *us. We* aren't Spry's enemies. We're his keepers. His caretakers. We want the best for him, just like you. Accordingly, in order to tailor our training methods to suit his needs, we must know how he's doing with the information we've given him. Like the scroll."

I began to feel dizzy. How much longer until seven minutes were up and I'd feel that rush of numb relief?

"Auricle, do you or do you not have any new intel to report on the matter?" Auld demanded, dropping the friendly façade.

"I-I don't. I haven't heard a thing, m-ma'am." I couldn't take any more of this. I needed to leave. Now.

"Very well, then," Auld's arms folded, floppy sleeves swinging, "if you *do* hear anything—verbally or spectrally—let us know, right away. That's an order. Do I make myself clear?"

An order. I gripped my armrests with both hands, dizziness progressing to full-on vertigo.

"A-are you asking me to s-spy on him, ma'am?" I squeaked.

Auld scoffed. "It isn't *spying;* we already told you, we're not his enemy. This is for his own good."

I was shaking now, this morning's porridge threatening to vacate my stomach in favor of my sandals.

"N-no, ma'am, spying is when anybody takes info from anybody else w-without their knowledge or consent. I-it doesn't matter who's doing it or w-what their intentions are."

Auld reached across her desk and grabbed me by the hair, yellow throat glowing. "Now, listen here, Useless," she hissed directly into my ear, words like a thousand fiery needles shooting through my scalp. "You will do as I say or you're Fire Pit kindle, got it?"

"M-ma'am, yes, ma'am," I whimpered.

She released me, sickening smile returning. "Now, go enjoy the first and last day off we'll ever let Spry grant you. Dismissed."

* * *

"Well, look who it is," Verteb Aqua announced as I strolled onto the taro fields for the first time since Summer Solstice Day. I fought the urge to wince as all my old friends yelped and bounded toward me; I'd forgotten how much noisier the civilian world was, compared to Fervor Base. "The prophet's ambassador has graced our shores; bow before him!"

I laughed. "It's so good to see all of you, again!"

Verteb grabbed my wrists. "Why, look at this," he half-shouted. "His palms are almost as smooth as yours, Apricot!" Immune to cuts, scrapes and dryness, Apricot's source was his skin. He was the only field-hand I knew without callouses. "Accustomed to the noble life now, are you?"

I gently pulled away. "What are you talking about, Verteb? I'm a servant."

"Uh huh, I bet you haven't pulled a single root since Summer Solstice Day, have you?" he bellowed.

This time, I couldn't help but flinch. My eardrums were still tender from Auld's fresh abuse. "Please, could you keep your voice down a bit? I'm really sore, right now."

"From what?" Verteb smirked. "Listening to the Icon turn the pages of his textbooks?"

Verteb didn't have a clue what base life entailed. Out here in the fields, there was no

looming international war, no terrible nightmares of blind babies and kitchen knives, no
haunting thoughts of a tormented military
captain filling my head, no knowledge of—
let alone willing rebellions against—the
Core Crystal, no high-ranking authorities
making death-threats if I failed to violate
my conscience on their command...

"What, you won't even talk to me, now?"
Verteb growled. "Too hoity-toity to answer
to a lowly peasant?"

"My boss just shouted at me," I whispered,
taken aback. "That's why I'm sore, okay?"

"Your boss," Verteb repeated. "You mean
the Icon?"

"No, Auld Pharynx, the Chief of Prophetic Affairs. Spry always keeps his voice
down around me; he'd never yell at me."

"Spry," he echoed, eyes full of scornful
disbelief. He turned to the others. "Listen
to that; Auricle's on a first-name basis with
the Multi-Source Enchant! *Spry* would
never yell at him!" He rounded on me. "You
should just call him what he *is*, Auricle. An
Icon. A tool. A privileged poster-boy who
doesn't know what it's like to sweat."

I was dumbfounded. "Of course, he knows what it's like to sweat." I looked at my friends' angry faces, wishing I could shout back without hurting myself. "He works just as hard as we all do, if not harder, studying and training. For Pekoe's sake, the System's about to send him off to war."

"Good," Verteb grunted, the other four nodding and chuckling in agreement. "Maybe, the Nordics will give his privileged silver ass what it deserves."

He was joking about a twenty-age-old getting killed in combat? I stared, astonished and sickened. "That'd be terrible. He's our age, Verteb. Do you hear yourself?"

"Do *you* hear *your*self? Pekoe, they've brainwashed you. The Auricle *I* know would be laughing with us, right now."

"Well, then, I guess the Auricle *you* know is dead," I shot, turning my back on them and stalking away.

"Sellout," Verteb called after me, loudly enough for the whole field to hear. "Guess you had a price, after all. You got bought, you traitorous piece of dragon dung."

I quickened my pace, hoping to get off the plantation before anyone could see the tears in my eyes. Through the spectral web, I could hear Kidni, Apricot, Tymp and Xero all echo Verteb's nasty thoughts and feelings toward me. No, 'nasty' was too mild a word. They downright hated me.

Since I relocated to Fervor ten days ago, I'd made one friend. But, in the process, I lost five.

SPRY SCINTILLATE

I held my quill with my teeth and fanned my parchment so the berry-ink would hurry up and dry, already. Due first thing in the morning, this Nordic Studies essay was supposed to fill an entire scroll. But, so far, I'd barely written a foot.

The door opened behind me. Hands, mouth and mind all preoccupied, I made no effort to acknowledge my visitor. I was used to having System admins come in at random times to observe me, taking tons of notes on Pekoe knew what. I'd learned to ignore them.

Then, I accidentally brought the ostrich-feather fan too close, smearing ink everywhere. Quill dropping from my lips, I swore at the top of my lungs. From behind me, someone inhaled sharply.

I swiveled around.

"Auricle?" I breathed. Auricle was curled up in his cot, facing away from me. If I'd known he was here, I wouldn't have shouted. "What are you doing back, already?" It was early evening.

"If it's really *my* day off, I can spend it however and *where*ver I want," he snapped.

"Of course," I answered, taken aback. "I just thought you would've had enough of holing up in this room, by now."

"Yeah, well," he drew his blanket, "just don't expect me to fix your supper, or anything."

I tossed my fan aside, forgetting all about 'The Effect of a Negligible Natural Carrying-Capacity on the Ichthyothian Socio-economic Climate.'

"What's going on?" I breathed. "Is everything alright?"

Silence.

"Auricle?"

"I'm going to sleep, *sir*. I don't have to answer to you, today."

I stared at his crooked back. "I'm not *ordering* you; I'm just worried." I really didn't like the idea that duty was the only reason Auricle ever spoke to me.

More silence.

Baffled, I returned to my work. But, the topic of Ichthyothian arctic adaptations seemed even less exciting than it was, mere seconds ago. I started recopying what I'd written thus far, since the original was all but a slimy mess.

What was wrong with Auricle? I gnawed the inside of my cheek. Today was supposed to be a good day, for him. The very last thing I expected was for him to return several hours early and in the worst mood I'd ever seen him in.

I turned back around. "Come on, man, just tell me what's up. Maybe, I can help."

He covered his ears, though I wasn't being loud. Which meant he wanted me to interpret the gesture as though coming from a non-ear-mage: shut up and leave me the hell alone.

I was already stressed photonless over the fact that my entire world had spiraled out of control in the last couple weeks alone, so I couldn't take Auricle's inexplicable anger, right now. I couldn't handle rejection from my only friend, not when I already felt abandoned and betrayed by my country. Not when I'd just learned that my whole life was a lie. Overcome by a caustic wave of frustration and fear and anger, I sprung up and kicked a hole right through my wooden wardrobe. Which made Auricle sit up, quick as gunfire. His face was red and scrunched and when he removed his palms from his ears, there was blood in them.

"Pekoe," I whispered, horrified. "Auricle, I'm so sorry; I didn't mean to—"

But, before I could say anything further, he fled the room.

It was well after midnight before I finished what was probably the worst essay in the history of System education.

* * *

"Auld wants to see you."

I opened my eyes. It was daybreak. Auricle stood at the foot of my bed, ears bandaged.

"Good morning," I told him, feebly.

He threw my silver robe at me with violent force.

"Hurry up and get to her office. She's not too happy."

"O-okay." I hoisted myself up. "What's going on?"

Silently, Auricle opened my door, stood to the side and bowed.

Taking the hint, I draped my robe over my pajamas and scurried down the corridor.

I entered Auld's office. Xon and Ala stood on either side of her.

"Sit down," Auld ordered stiffly, without so much as a 'good day.'

I sat.

"So, you've been having nightmares," she cut straight to business. "Terrible, graphic visions involving the blinding of the Ichthyothian Diving Captain."

I froze, careful not to let the shock show on my face. I didn't dare deny it. It wasn't worth the mental effort. I had a hunch that I needed to save my steam for whatever was about to go down.

"You feel sorry for him," Auld continued, tone biting and mocking. "You cried for him. You wish you could've saved him from his parents. You wish you could give him back his sight." She raised her voice, which was no mere matter for a throat mage: "He, your enemy who'd kill you at first glance!"

I looked away.

"Pitying him doesn't make you a hero. It doesn't make you noble. It doesn't make you righteous. It just makes you a *fool*. An irresponsible, soft-hearted, cowardly *fool*." She leaned in. "You are the Multi-Source Enchant. Do you know what that means? You're *it*. The only chance we've got. There's more on the line here than your life or the lives of a couple hundred soldiers. If you fail, *Conflagria* fails. If you fail, *your nation* is condemned forever to obscurity in this world. Do you understand? What happened to Terminus Lechatelierite when he was a child was unfortunate, yes. But, it's nothing compared to what'll happen to this *entire island* if you continue to let your *feelings* derail your focus and destroy your resolve. The future of magekind is in your hands, Spry. Wake the hell up!"

I studied the cracks in the stone beneath my feet, face burning hotter than a hobnail's throat. There was only one way that Auld could've known any of this: Auricle. Auricle's lifeline was twined to mine, and his extraordinary magic made him privy to some of the secrets in my head.

It made no sense. Auricle was my friend. Why would my friend betray me?

* * *

I skipped breakfast. Instead, I went back to my quarters, where I found Auricle methodically making my bed.

"Hey," I said, shutting the door behind me, "we need to talk."

He finished carefully tucking the corners of the sheets before turning to face me.

"What about, sir?" he asked, bowing.

I sleeve-wiped my sweaty forehead. If *one more* person bowed to me and called me 'sir,' I was going to crack. "You've been acting weird since you returned yesterday. Something's obviously upsetting you, and I need to know what it is. Did I screw up, somehow? Is everything alright, back home? Please, I can't help you, if you shut me out."

"I don't need your help, sir," he said, bowing again.

That was it. I was done playing nice. "Why did you sell me out to Auld?" I snapped. "For Pekoe's sake, Auricle, I thought we were friends."

He blinked. "What gave you that idea, sir?" Rendered speechless now, I stared at his emotionless face for several drawn-out seconds. Then, at a total loss of what to do next, I numbly walked over to my desk, sat down and put my head in my hands.

He watched me impassively for a few moments then went back to work, stuffing my dirty laundry into a wicker basket. When he passed right by me, I suddenly sprang up, kicking it right out of his arms.

"You know what *gave me that idea?*" I snarled, pushing him into a wall. Fear flashed across his face. "Ignorance. I never knew what it's like to have a friend; I'd never had one before. Sure, I've got a whole nation full of people who know my name, but they don't give a damn about *me*. They just worship the phony hero the System's made out of me."

I raised my voice: "Even so, I still thought I knew what a friend's *supposed* to be like—someone who sees beyond titles and labels." I laughed, bitterly. "Maybe, I am a fool, like Auld said. A fool to ever think I'd find somebody *real* on this godforsaken island."

I grabbed my diving suit from my wardrobe and headed out to practice, white-hot rage pulsing through my legs and hair like spectrum of the wrong frequency. I spent twenty ages believing that loyalty and compassion were the default human behaviors, not hostility and enmity. Was I naïve to think that there was more good than bad on Second Earth? Did I have too much hope in mankind? I was supposed to be a prophet, a savior. But, what kind of world was I saving?

TERMINUS LECHATELIERITE

Some people just had the 'hero look.' Broad shoulders, a bulky build, windswept hair, white teeth. As I sat before my computer now, perusing a new report from the Ichthyothian Intelligence Agency, it became glaringly apparent to me that System Water Forces Captain Spry Skii Scintillate was one of those people.

It wasn't too hard for the IIA to dig up information on Scintillate—the kid was a sensation all across Conflagria. His picture and story were everywhere. The Ichthyothian media liked to *talk* a lot about me, but my photo hardly ever circulated. It didn't take a social scientist to figure that a half-blind, small-statured kid wouldn't bolster public confidence in the military.

I studied Scintillate's picture. His hair was startlingly silver. His frame was large and well-muscled, especially his legs. His skin was bronze and stretched tight over his high cheekbones and strong jaw. His gold-green eyes were bright and sharp, framed by long grey lashes.

His life story was just as I expected. Born an only child to wealthy parents on Summer Solstice Day of the eighty-seventh age, his multi-sources—legs and hair—were confirmed at his Circle Trial at age six. He grew up in his parents' palace in the suburban outskirts of Ardor Village until he was made Captain of the System Water Forces on his twentieth birthday, a couple weeks ago.

I refused to be intimidated by Scintillate's stature or spectral gifts. To the Conflagrians, his hotshot look made him easy to love. For me, it made him easy to hate. I was glad the IIA delivered this report to me. It gave me a distinct target for my anger. A name and face.

As I met his smarmy golden-green gaze, I wondered what magekind would think of their prophet after a one-hundred-pound one-eyed Nordic finished him off.

PART II
THE FIRST WAR

I knew a simple solder boy
Who grinned at life in empty joy,
Slept soundly through the lonesome dark,
And whistled early with the lark.

In winter trenches, cowed and glum,
With cramps and lice and lack of rum,
He put a bullet through his brain.
No one spoke of him again.

You smug-faced crowds with kindling eye
Who cheer when soldier lads march by,
Sneak home and pray you'll never know
The hell where youth and laughter go.

—"Suicide in the Trenches" *by Siegfried Sassoon*

TERMINUS LECHATELIERITE

July seventh of the seventh age, seventh era was a monumental day of discovery in the field of Ichthyothian spectroscopy.

Ichthyosis was supposed to be on the defensive in the forthcoming war—the Conflagrians were the aspiring conquistadors, here. So, all we'd been doing since discovering their hostile intentions was training and waiting readily for them to make a move. We figured that there was nothing to be gained from striking first and picking fights earlier than necessary.

Until now.

For ages, the IIA aimed its long-range spectroscopes—space satellites and landbound radars alike—at the island, monitoring the activity of the spectral web. The project was controversial and unpopular; the public at large was of the opinion that it was a waste of time and resources, as we weren't able to make much sense of anything we detected. The readings just looked like a crazy jumble of wavelengths. Frequencies redshifted and blueshifted all over the place, but none of it meant a damn thing to us.

In the past week, however, a handful of IIA physicists decided to try something different. Instead of just passively recording frequencies, they started dispersing radiant energy *into* the web, 'plucking' strands at random.

Resultingly, a rather peculiar phenomenon got discovered: an unusually dense concentration of magic, at the center of the web. It was hypothesized that most, if not all, mage auras touched at this point. It was the fulcrum of the entire electromagnetic spectrum.

The wavelength at the core of the cluster was stronger and brighter than the rest. And, it was silver. The conclusion was obvious; that hearty line belonged to the Multi-Source Enchant.

Immediately, the experimenters grew cautious. They figured that it was a bad idea to pluck Spry Scintillate's line directly, because they had reason to believe he'd detect the intrusion. However, they figured that it was unlikely that normal single-sourced mages would be as receptive or aware. So, they sought to pluck the lines most tightly twined to Scintillate's. There weren't many to choose from. Apparently, the Multi-Source Enchant was a lonely man, lifeline only tied to three others: a purple, a blue, and, most tightly, a yellow. These were the individuals in closest emotional proximity to our target.

Emotional proximity. That was the problem. There was no guarantee those *emotionally* closest to Scintillate were also *physically* nearest to him. By regularly plucking the trio of lines, we were able to keep tabs on the coordinates of Scintillate's three friends. But, not the man himself.

Like all frequencies, the purple and blue spectra shifted all the time. Though, more often than not, they could still be traced to a palace in the suburbs of Ardor Village. It was determined that these were probably Scintillate's parents. The yellow line was far more interesting. It tended to stay along the Fervor coast, where the System recently established a military base. This seemed like a more probable location for Scintillate.

As for the cluster itself, it never redshifted nor blueshifted. Which meant its location was fixed.

I set our infiltration date for July twenty-fifth. We had two objectives: to destroy the cluster and kill Scintillate.

TERMINUS LECHATELIERITE

It was the eve of our strike. My fleet and I were making our way across the Briny Ocean in a vitreous silica and a dozen crystallines. We planned to travel through the night and attack just before dawn.

As far as we knew, the enemy was completely in the dark about our advance. But, of course, I still had to have plan 'B.'

For security reasons, the IIA only ever dared to lightly probe and pluck lifelines in the web. But, of course, their spectrometers were capable of dispersing much stronger waves of radiant energy than they'd used, thus far—so strong, in fact, that the impact could kill. So, without seeking the approval of the Trilateral Committee, I got an IIA physics lackey—Dimi Utive, a sophomore at Crystal University who interned at the agency headquarters in Nox City—to agree to man a thirty-six-meter, small-angle, neuron-scattering satellite spectrometer, on my mark. So, if the Conflagrians met us in the sea, their fleet stood no chance.

Unfortunately, however, this weapon couldn't be tested in advance, because it wasn't exactly discreet. Trying it out early would undoubtedly tip off the enemy. I preferred if the Conflagrians remained ignorant of our ability to manipulate the visible spectrum, fighting fire with fire.

As we traveled, I continued to monitor the three wavelengths twined to Scintillate using the on-board spectrometer, which wasn't nearly as refined nor powerful as those possessed by the IIA. The IIA's spectrometers sufficed with a single 'pluck' per strand per day, to keep tabs. But, with *this* lousy unit, I had to send out the signal, almost continually. So far, so good, though—none of them had blueshifted nor redshifted, all night. They were still as stones. Probably sound asleep in their beds.

Sleep tight, savages, I thought. I'm coming for you.

* * *

Hours passed and my soldiers were trying hard to hide their anxiety. Even I was a bit nervous about making the initial strike against the System, thereby starting the very first war in Second Earth history.

There was a lot of talk among my men in the corridors of the vitreous silica. Talk, not only about the risks involving blacklisting, but about how we didn't really know *what* we were about to attack, when it came to the fulcrum. What would a dense concentration of spectrum *look* like? A big ball of colorful light? I sincerely hoped not. I'd prefer if it were a finite physical entity that could be shattered.

The IIA hypothesized that most mages would be weakened if we destroyed or damaged the cluster. How, exactly, we didn't know. Would they die? Possibly, the physicists said, but we shouldn't count on it. Would they lose their magical powers? The scientific community determined that was far more likely.

But, I had a different idea. My thoughts kept circling back to the Conflagrian social complacency issue—the inexplicable docility of the entire mage population despite their government's obvious corruption. I wondered if the cluster had anything to do with *that*.

AURICLE CAPITULUM

I rolled over in my cot, eardrums pounding as throbs of radiant energy bombarded my aura. I'd heard it occasionally, in the past—the stabbing sensation of a spectrometer yanking my wavelength—but, never at such an intensity as this. I writhed in my sheets, fighting the urge to call out. I knew that screaming would only add to the chaos and make everything worse.

"Any redshifts or blueshifts, Buird?" came an unfamiliar male voice.

"Blue, purple and yellow are all still stable, sir. Probably asleep."

"Good. Keep an especially close eye on the yellow; he's the important one."

The words were harsh, consonant. Not Conflagrian. Ichthyothian? It had to have been. And, yet, I could understand them. How?

Yellow one.

Redshifts and blueshifts.

Ichthyothian.

Holy Pekoe.

"He's fairly far from the fulcrum."

"Yes, the energy cluster is inland, whereas the yellow lifeline can be traced to the Fervor shore. Doesn't exactly make things easy for us."

"Sir, do you think they'll die, if we disrupt the cluster?"

"No. It'll probably weaken or disable their powers, though. And, maybe…"

There was a pause.

"Sir?"

"Forget it, Buird."

A cluster. A fulcrum that sustained our powers. The Core Crystal. So, the Ichthyothians knew. They knew, and they were on their way now, to find it. The Nordics had grown tired of waiting for us to strike first. They decided to declare war themselves, before we were ready. Spry wasn't finished with his training. He couldn't use his second source, yet.

"Nox City, do you copy?"

"Roger, Captain. Spectrometer seven-two-five is online and ready for transmission. Shockwave will launch, on your mark."

"Easy, there, Utive. We're still twenty minutes out. For now, just sit tight, stay alert and pray that I won't need a damn thing from you, after all."

"Yes, sir."

I sat up, nauseous and sweaty. "Spry," I murmured weakly, barely able to hear my own voice above the ringing in my ears.

I looked over at his bed. It was empty. He must've been in the barracks, with his men. Sometimes, he slept there, when evening practice ran late.

I tumbled from my cot, dizzy and disoriented. Upon my arrival at Fervor Base, Auld had sternly ordered me to stay out of any and all military affairs. She said that I had neither the intelligence nor the right to interfere in war matters.

But, here I was, holding Conflagria's future in my hands, anyway.

As the world spun before my eyes, I crawled on my hands and knees down the dark corridors, balance totally shot by the throbbing in my inner ear. At last, swallowing a mouthful of vomit, I slapped the door to the barracks with an open palm.

After a minute that felt more like an era, it swung open, revealing a short brutish-looking mage with olive-green hands.

"Spry," I panted. "I n-need to see Spry."

"The *Captain* is asleep," he shot, looking down at me with contemptuous eyes.

"Please, w-wake him." Stomach acid burned my throat. "I-it's an emergency."

The man just pursed his lips and scowled.

"Hurry," I wheezed. "There's no time to waste—we're all in serious danger. The Ichthyothians are almost here."

"Is this some sort of joke, Useless?" he spat.

"What's going on, over there?" Spry called from somewhere inside.

At the sound of Spry's voice, I felt an intense surge of relief. Of all people, Spry would take me seriously. I wasn't just a Useless to him; I was his friend. His confidante. He listened to me.

I hoped.

"Spry," I spoke as loud as I could—barely above a whisper, at this point. "Spry, the Ichthyothians are coming; you've got to hurry!"

"Looks like your little servant had a nightmare, Captain," the green mage growled. "Capitulum, apologize for disturbing your master," he ordered me.

"Please," I choked into the growing hubbub. The room buzzed with the grunts of angry sleep-deprived men. "Please, listen to me. I d-didn't have a nightmare. I heard a... d-disturbance, in the spectrum."

Spry appeared in the doorframe, massive arms folded. "What's the matter, Auricle?" he asked, quietly.

"Spry!" I cried, adrenaline and magic rapidly giving me the second wind I desperately needed. "Spry, the Ichthyothians are just miles from the shore. They're after the Core Crystal. They don't know what it is, but they can sense its energy. And, they have a spectrometer—one that can send killer shockwaves through the air and sea."

Spry took in the news without so much as a blink. He turned.

"Attention," he called to his men, face as stoic as ever. "To the hangar, immediately!"

At Spry's orders, there was an explosion of hubbub—soldiers throwing off covers, jumping from bunks, stripping off pajamas, pulling on wetsuits.

Pawing the doorframe, I pulled myself upright. "You... you listened to me," I breathed to Spry.

He regarded me with placid eyes. "Of course I did, Auricle." He blinked, solemnly. "Why wouldn't I?"

I looked away, ashamed.

The green mage—now dressed in combat attire whose markings revealed that he was second-in-line to Spry—addressed his Captain directly: "Sir, I believe that all hair mages should surface-ride. If the Nordics use the shockwave, they can weave their locks into a net to rebound the energy." His knuckles cracked. "Your hair can be the primary line of defense, with the rest serving as reinforcement."

Spry's face betrayed nothing. "Yes, all hair-mages will surface-ride," was all he said.

SPRY SCINTILLATE

I ran out into the hangar, the white face of the Ichthyothian Diving Captain haunting my mind's eye. I pictured the slash that bisected his liquid stare. It was like a line of fire slicing through the cobalt-blue sea itself.

I don't want to kill you, I thought, imagining his childishly-smooth cheeks and rumpled hair. Please, don't make me kill you.

SPRY SCINTILLATE

I hooked my toes on the rungs of Oliver's dragon ship to give my fingers a break. I always found it easier to surface-ride with my feet. The flippers got in the way sometimes, but even so, it was easier than using my hands.

And, far easier than trying to use my hair.

I was supposed to be the most powerful mage in Conflagrian history. While my leg-magic was definitely above average, my hair was still dormant. Until today, no one outside the Pekoe administration knew, except Auricle. Not even my comrades.

Auld once explained to me the phenomenon of source-dormancy. It was a known spectral condition, however rare. While Infrareds were thought to be doomed to an indefinitely magicless existence, Dormants had hope of recovery. They potentially could, in their lifetimes, exercise their auras and eventually become decent mages. On some occasions, all a dormant limb needed to grow usable was an 'activator.' A spark. Something to shock it to life. Something to wake it up. An emergency that'd trigger a serious surge of adrenaline and spectrum.

Well, if a great big deadly shockwave launched by a gigantic Ichthyothian spectrometer didn't qualify as an emergency, nothing would. Right?

I shifted on Oliver's rungs and realized that, in my anxiety, I'd been gnawing the inside of my cheek—my mouth tasted bitter. If my hair magic was working, the little wound would've healed before it got the chance to really bleed.

I couldn't believe that the war was mere hours old and we'd already lost our only advantage, our only edge—the one thing we had that the enemy didn't. The ability to wield magic.

Lechatelierite. No doubt, all this was his idea. The System had long since been aware of his dangerous interest in spectroscopy. But, instead of preparing appropriately, extrapolating what spectral scheme he may conjure up in combat, what did they do? They stupidly chose to believe that the Childhood Program would have snuffed out his curiosity by now. Of course, the CP failed at that. Some people were just born to color outside the lines, against all odds.

The Ichthyothian crafts—salted with the bodies of the white-suited surface-riders—were now within eyeshot.

"Captain," Oliver's voice rang in my helmet, laden with dread, "Captain, they've launched it already. The shockwave is coming for us." He gave me the current coordinates and the (rather rapid) rate of approach.

Stomach twisting like a typhoon, I unclenched my jaw and gave the orders I knew could very well be my last. Our vessels circled up as the hair mages weaved their locks into a lattice, seven miles in diameter—four below the surface and three above. And, at the center of it all was me, riding atop Oliver's dragon ship, framed by the hairy backboard, presumably ready to lash out my own hair at exactly the right moment, absorbing the brunt of the blow.

Either that or we'd all instantly die upon contact, giving the Nordics a clean shot to infiltrate the island and attack the Core Crystal.

Then, a voice in the back of my mind hissed: would that really be so bad?

Stop it, Spry, I silently scolded myself. I couldn't afford to think like that at a time like this! Everyone was counting on me. Like it or not, ready or not, this was what I was born for. My whole life came down to this moment.

As though the sea were a vat of oil set ablaze, the shockwave advanced. Poking my head above water, I threw off my helmet, hairs on the back of my neck already standing up—but, from fear, not spectrum.

Oliver's voice boomed: "Impact in ten... nine..."

Adrenaline and spectrum smoldered in my muscles, as though my heart pumped pure acid.

"Eight... seven... six..."

My aura shone brighter than ever before; a scintillating silver mist permeated the air and danced upon the rippling waves.

"Five... four... three..."

It was now or never. Screaming, I tossed my head forward.

"Two… one… NOW!"

Alas, my hair remained still as a sack of taro. So, instinctively, I leaned back, doubling my legs under me. As colorful flashes filled my sight, my whole body went hot, as though tossed into the Fire Pit itself.

The rainbow of light turned to black.

* * *

I lay on my side, hacking like a thunderstorm, legs still locked in position. Dimly aware of the fiery agony tormenting my every cell and photon, I opened my eyes.

Apparently, I'd washed up on shore. How? Moaning, I threw up once, twice, three times. Pawing the sand, I slowly sat up and stared out to sea.

The surface was cluttered with floating bodies. Hundreds of white and orange corpses bobbled in the current, helmets knocking into one another, suits waxy in the blazing sun. It was glaringly obvious that every single surface-rider who deployed today, Ichthyothian and Conflagrian alike, was dead.

Except me.

Lechatelierite had sorely underestimated his own weapon.

With a mechanical hum, the sea regurgitated a heavily-damaged crystalline onto the beach, only a couple dozen yards away from me. And, with a single pop, I could suddenly see through the center of my right palm.

I inhaled, sharply. Someone shot a freaking *hole* through my *hand?*

Sure enough, an enemy diver—the pilot of the half-demolished shuttle—was running my way, wielding a sidearm. I reached for my own weapon and was horrified to find my entire utility belt missing; it must've gotten swept up in the tide. Forgetting all about my aching muscles and gunshot wound—fueled with the superhuman urgency of a soldier staring down death—I leapt to my feet, sprinted toward my attacker and kicked his gun right out of his fist, snapping it in two.

At that point, I expected him to flee. An unarmed Nordic should know better than to try to wrestle a mage, even an injured one. Ichthyothians, without all their fancy tech, didn't really stand a chance against magic, when it came to hand-to-hand combat.

Or, so, I thought.

Physically, the diver was petite—and not just compared to me. Standing upright, his head barely reached my belly, and his entire frame seemed slighter than a single thigh of mine. While littleness was typically considered a handicap in a fight, this guy—with his lightening-quick twirls and summersaults—certainly knew how to work it. No matter what I did, I couldn't seem to land a single blow.

Dodging a kick now, the Nordic dropped to the sand, rolling to my right. And, using my bulk in the most unorthodox way imaginable, I gave into the spontaneous urge to turn and sit on him.

His tiny frame collapsed under my tremendous weight. He was trapped.

I was stunned that my silly move actually worked. The Ichthyothian was so nimble, I half-expected to wind up landing in the sand as he flipped over my head. It was like he just flat-out didn't see me come at him, on his left.

Oh.

Of course.

I stared into his visor. Sure enough, my gaze was met by one sapphire eye and one half-closed, cloudy, bisected orb.

Captain Terminus Lechatelierite.

I gasped, audibly. Conflagria's greatest enemy was completely at my mercy. The leader of the Diving Fleet. The one Nordic who was daring and ruthless enough to try to wield magic against mages. I could stomp his tiny ribcage with my boot, right now. It'd be so easy. It'd decapitate the entire Ichthyothian Resistance. It'd transform this disastrous battle into a solid strike against the enemy.

But, as I watched his pale face redden, all I could think about was his mother brandishing a kitchen knife while his father egged her on. And, the Childhood Program that brainwashed him since infancy. And, the Trilateral Committee that threw him, at the tender age of nineteen, on the frontlines of the first international war in Second Earth history—the war that only got started in the first place because Principal Pekoe decided that he wanted to be a conquistador. And, of twelve-age-old Auricle crumpling beneath his supervisor's vicious blows. And, of the secret of the Core Crystal that daily filled me with rage and sorrow and lethargy.

I didn't believe in the cause I was fighting for. I didn't stand for the orange and green on my own back. And, I'd be damned if I caused one more man to die for Pekoe's criminal crusade.

I heaved myself up from Lechatelierite's trembling body. Surprisingly, rather than attacking, he made a beeline for the shore, diving headfirst into the sea.

I didn't follow.

AURICLE CAPITULUM

The Ichthyothian Diving Fleet—or, what was left of it, anyway—retreated after deploying the shockwave, lacking the manpower to infiltrate the island and attack the Core Crystal, as they'd originally planned. So, technically, the Nordics didn't win the first battle of the Ichthyo-Conflagrian War.

But, neither did the System.

I'd like to say that Spry took it all very well—that he jumped right back on the dragon with a renewed thirst for the Conflagrian crusade.

But, I'd be lying.

Until the disaster of July twenty-fifth, the System believed that it was only a matter of time before Spry's second source awakened. But, after watching his hair magic fail so spectacularly even in the direst of situations, it became evident that this was no temporary phase: the dormancy of his locks was a permanent affliction. Spry wasn't the Multi-Source Enchant.

With above-average leg-magic but only a useless photon flicker in his hair, the man was a spectral phenomenon unlike anything Conflagria had seen before. 'Partial-multi-sourced' was the new term. Spry was the first of his kind. He was a mutant. A freak. Unnatural. Inhuman.

Branded a 'false prophet,' Spry was discharged from the Water Forces. As his court-martial approached, he didn't prepare to litigate, though his life was literally on the line. In fact, he didn't do much of anything anymore, besides sleep. Not because he was tired. He was broken.

I knew it wasn't the public humiliation that ultimately shattered Spry's resolve. Despite his lifetime in the limelight, he never actually cared for status nor reputation. No, I believed what truly crushed his spirit was watching the vast majority of his army die in the wake of his failure. And, coming dangerously close to killing Lechatelierite, whom he saw as a person—a person he related to and cared about—rather than a faceless 'enemy.'

Some soldiers, Lechatelierite probably among them, could stomach the grisliness of combat without crumbling. But, others just couldn't, no matter what; it wasn't necessarily a matter of training, but personality. It turned out, Spry simply couldn't be desensitized, despite how much he studied the art of war. He couldn't distance his heart from his duty. Sure, he was able to perform well in training, when no real blood got spilled. But, that didn't mean he could stand real carnage.

Knowing Spry hadn't prepared a legal defense, I decided to show up at his trial intending to fight for his life, all on my own. Walking in, I was worried that I'd be dismissed simply because I was an uneducated Useless. But, interestingly enough, the judges allowed me on the stand without much objection.

And, by the third day of the proceedings, I noticed a change in my ear magic.

Never before had I concentrated so hard for so long on anything. Never before did I have a real reason to, having been cast aside so early in life. Since early childhood, my world mostly consisted of harvesting taro. I was never intellectually nor spectrally challenged. I was never motivated to exert myself mentally nor magically.

Until now. Because I cared more for the outcome of Spry's court-martial than I did for the Ichthyo-Conflagrian war itself. So, I concentrated hard and, in the process, finally discovered the difference between listening and hearing.

Since birth, I'd done nothing but hear. Everything. All the time. But, I never really listened. I didn't think I could. After all, my magic was uncontrolled, unrefined. Continually overwhelmed by the hubbub of my surroundings, I thought it futile to even try to pick up on people's subtle vocal inflections. Yet, the more I listened to Spry's opponents in court—focusing intently on the textures of their voices—the more I found myself able to tune out the noise pollution. And, since most of their silent thoughts pertained to Spry, my aura was open to detecting many of those too, giving me a unique edge in debate.

I guessed my source wasn't so useless, after all.

In the end, though Spry was still universally despised and disgraced, he got off with his life. He was permitted to quietly gather his things and go home. Not to Fervor.

As for me, my service on base was also through. I no longer had anyone to wait on. It was back to the taro fields. All my old friends, even Verteb Aqua, reaccepted me without a glimpse of grief. I supposed that they didn't envy the Icon or his shadow so much, anymore.

TERMINUS LECHATELIERITE

War was a lot harder than it looked. It was easy to read First Earth accounts and *think* you'd know what to do in their place. But, when it came to the actual practical execution of the theoretical concepts we'd studied, Ichthyosis apparently had a lot to learn. Mistakes were made by pretty much every party involved in the implementation and execution of our inaugural battle. The Trilateral Committee. The Ichthyothian Intelligence Agency. My men. Me.

For one, Ichthyosis shouldn't have made the first move, after all. The TC decided that we wouldn't take provocative offensive action against Conflagria again, unless absolutely necessary. We were the Ichthyothian *Resistance,* and we were going to act like it from now on, merely guarding our turf from mage imperialism, defending our-selves from *their* strikes until they eventual-ly realized the futility of their conquistador aspirations.

The IIA also determined that it was a bad idea to pluck lifelines with spectrometers, no matter how gentle or infrequent. How else did the System discover our advance? Our entire battle-strategy hinged on the belief that only the Multi-Source Enchant could detect subtle activity in the web. Boy, were we wrong. Whoever owned the yellow line managed to sense our presence loud and clear, enabling the System Water Forces to prep for our strike. So, we couldn't disrupt auras like that, ever again.

As for me, my battle plan was a total bust, from top to bottom. I failed at achieving our objectives: killing Scintillate and destroying the cluster, whatever it was. With the shockwave, I did wipe out most of the Water Forces… but, with it, went my surface-riders. Every last one of them.

"You ought to be court-martialed for this."

I now stood before Sergeant Irri's desk, staring at the white metal floor.

"I warned you not to tamper with spectroscopy; I *warned* you!" He got to his feet, towering threateningly. "I thought you got your head out of the clouds ages ago, Terminus. If the TC had any idea that you were still dabbling in that hocus-pocus nonsense all this time, they never would've let you graduate into the fleet, let alone give you the captaincy."

I swallowed.

"Dimi Utive, the intern you put up to this shockwave fiasco," Irri's arms folded, "has been fired from the IIA and expelled from Crystal University." Irri began pacing, furiously. "But, the education and career of a civilian teenager is the least of our worries, right now—the mess you made has wrecked far more lives than his."

I spoke to my boots, "I'm sorry, sir. I underestimated the shockwave's destructive force. I didn't anticipate its amplification upon reflection from the hair-mages' net."

"Hell, it's almost as if you set off a nuclear bomb," Irri barked. From what I'd read about nuclear explosives in First Earth history, I was pretty sure that Irri's comparison wasn't even remotely accurate, but I wasn't about to correct him. "And, you know why you couldn't guess what your little spectral tsunami would do?" He raised his voice: "Because the supernatural is neither logical nor predictable." He stopped pacing, fists balled at his sides. "We're Nordics, Terminus. We don't play with magic. We wield science. Technology. Physics. Mathematics. We work with what makes *sense*. What we can control. I never want to see you—or anyone in our military—use a spectrometer like that again. Understood?"

"Sir, yes, sir."

Irri sat down heavily, at his desk. "Dismissed," he tiredly breathed.

I dared to raise my gaze an inch. That was it? I broke the law, killed over half my fleet and escaped with my life only because Spry Scintillate inexplicably went soft on me when face-to-face… and all I got was a slap on the wrist?

Irri opened his laptop and began typing away, ignoring me. I didn't go. I just stood there, transfixed.

Without even glancing my way, he answered my unvoiced question: "No, Terminus, we're neither discharging nor demoting you. Yes, what you did was incredibly irresponsible and stupid," his eyes lifted from the screen, "but, it was also inventive and daring."

What? My lips parted.

"However, Terminus," he went on, "the key to success in combat is finding a balance. There's a fine line between crazy and creative, and an even finer one between reckless and brave. I trust that, from here on out, you'll know where to draw those lines."

I couldn't believe my ears. I didn't dare move, speak or even blink.

"Don't let us down again, soldier," he said, stonily. "You're still the best we've got."

AURICLE CAPITULUM

Months passed since Spry's court-martial, and I saw nothing of him. I went to his place many times, but his parents always turned me away. I understood Spry's desire to hide from the world at large, but I expected to be the one exception to that rule. I was his best friend, for Pekoe's sake; what did I do to deserve to be shut out? Oh, yes: I saved his life. The life he hated.

Worse yet, my ability to hear him through the web was already fading. I received fuzzy blips every now and then, but that was it. I didn't know if that was because Spry was losing his mind, or because our frequencies were starting to unravel from one another, or both.

Of course, the silence made me sad. But, moreover, it made me afraid. I could only hope that Spry's death-wishes were quieted because he was healing, not because I just couldn't hear them anymore.

* * *

The System 'resurfaced' the spectral web to wipe all memory of the war from the minds of the masses. Soldiers (and those who served them, like me) were obviously exempt, though strictly forbidden to babble. Not that we easily could anyway, thanks to the Core Crystal. Though the System intended to continue the conflict and even publicly maintain a military, the war itself would stay concealed from the masses, until victory was declared. In the meantime, mages would only learn about it upon enlistment.

The System had many rationales for this decision, the first of which was the over-taxation of the Core Crystal since the war's outbreak. Though the anti-war sentiment couldn't manifest itself in anything more than scattered seven-minute bursts of anger, the sheer number of people experiencing these moments of defiant rage still put a serious strain on the spectral web. And, so, the System sought to quell all public discontentment by eliminating knowledge of the war, altogether.

The second reason was to save face. The System wasn't supposed to make mistakes, yet their biggest project—Spry Scintillate—turned out to be a big one. So, as far as everyone knew now, Spry was immediately recognized as a 'partial-multi-sourced mage' at his Circle Trial, ages ago. His true tragic tale would never be told again.

The System decided Spry's memory should also be wiped, though he wasn't a civilian. But, when they tried to manipulate their ex-prophet's aura, they failed. His powerful frequency apparently made him immune. So, he was doomed to live the rest of his life in the shadow of his past.

The System resented the twenty ages of time and energy they'd spent on Spry and decided to make his family pay for it. Stripped of their fine possessions and lofty social status, they were forced from their palace in favor of a tiny cabin in Ardor Village, along the Dust Path. Spry was assigned to work on a flea-ridden sugar-cane plantation on the far side of town. I'd much rather pull taro.

Turned out, I was the fortunate one, after all. Not because my labor was gentler than Spry's, but because I never fell the way he did. I never had power nor prestige to begin with; since birth, I simply had no lower tier to descend to. But, Spry? Spry tumbled from the top of a tall tower. He had everything to lose, and he wound up losing it. People like me could never know how that felt.

I was sure of one thing, though: I wasn't really useless. My ear magic saved Spry's life. Twice. From the Nordics, our enemy in the war... and from a second, unexpected enemy—his own keepers.

War was consuming the northwestern hemisphere. Conflagria was a playground of classism and prejudice. The world was full of isolationistic racism. There was so much work to be done. Everywhere, there were problems that desperately needed solving, lives that needed saving.

Well, I saved one man. Just one. But, that was enough. That was far more than this Useless peasant ever thought he could accomplish in his lifetime.

EPILOGUE

"He who saves one life saves the world entire."
—Babylonian Talmud

Ages passed and the 'First War,' as the world eventually came to know it, dragged on. And, because the world did indeed come to know it by the onset of the 'Second War' ages later, North Ichthyosis—the longtime leader of the Second Earth Order—got blacklisted. The ice island was therefore left with only one trade partner: a large peninsular nation just a thousand or so miles south, across the Septentrion Sea. The Democratic-Republic of Nuria received special permission from the Free Peoples of Oriya, the new Order Authority, to maintain its trade-license with Ichthyosis because, without it, the super-power would be starved of oil. Although the Ichthyothian economy and quality of life drooped considerably upon blacklisting, its special commercial relationship with Nuria saved it from total demise.

Meanwhile, roughly three-thousand miles from those troubled snowy shores, a disenfranchised Ex-Multi-Source Enchant was trying to figure out what to do with himself. Deemed more useless than the Uselesses, he was assigned to a sugar-cane plantation and eventually ordered to marry a far-younger bird-boned woman named Turq Oibis who had hollow cheeks, large eyes and long magical hair. The townsfolk liked to laugh and joke about how Spry could easily crush his tiny turquois wife like a scarab if he rolled over in his sleep.

Turq—knowledge of the war vanquished—could never really understand why her tall, dark, handsome husband was always so downcast. Neither could he tell her, thanks to the Core Crystal, whose dominion he no longer had the strength to actively oppose. So, Spry lived with his past painfully bottled up, and Turq lived haunted by the suspicion that her partner was hiding something from her. The secret war cast a permanent shadow over their home.

Spry didn't want children, but his wife—desperate to add some coherence to their rocky relationship—insisted. They bickered for ages until finally, at age fifty, Spry relented. And so, Coronate Regal, named for the color purple, was born. Unfortunately for Auricle Capitulum—Spry's former servant and only remaining friend—the baby was a throat mage.

Spry was relieved that his son was definitively single-sourced. Despite Turq's tearful pleading, no more children were born to their household. The aged veteran was too afraid of siring a mage with his so-called 'gifts.'

Auricle Capitulum also married and had a son. That son was named Palli Tress for his fine white hair, and he made his father very proud. Like Spry, Auricle also refused to have children after Palli. He didn't want to risk bringing a Useless into the world.

Despite all he'd witnessed at Fervor Base in his youth, Auricle remained a patriot his entire life, rarely experiencing seven-minute blips of defiance. His family boasted a strong pro-System ideology. Accordingly, when Palli grew up, he planted the same values in his own progeny. Auricle's grand-daughter, also a white hair-mage, was called to serve in the Water Forces at age ten. Her name was Fair Gabardine. The old ear mage couldn't have been prouder.

The same month that Fair began her military training, Auricle died peacefully at home, from spinal-fluid leak. He remained cheerful on his deathbed, thankful that he got to live long enough to see his child and grandchild prosper. He passed away with a smile lingering on his lips.

He outlived his former master, Spry Scintillate, by nearly a decade, but thankfully, that wasn't long enough for him to get to witness his beloved granddaughter turn against the System and co-lead the island's first revolution.

* * *

In the seventeenth age of the seventh era, Captain Terminus Lechatelierite was awarded a Silver Triangle, the highest honor a diver could receive. At thirty, he hadn't lost a single battle since that infamous inaugural fight on July twenty-fifth of the seventh age.

Twenty ages later, at fifty, Terminus retired and was finally permitted to start a family. Heart hardened by decades of carnage, he married for the wrong reason: the Trilateral Committee wanted another Lechatelierite child. They demanded it. Everyone believed that any offspring of the great Diving Captain would likely inherit his talent for war. And, so, in the fortieth age of the seventh era, the ex-soldier bent once again to the will of those who raised him and had a son with his much-younger wife, Christallina Aveline.

The child's name was Finis Arrete Lechatelierite and he was nothing special. An average boy. The Diving Fleet didn't have room for average boys. At only three ages old, Finis was expelled from the Childhood Program and sent home.

And, so, Terminus suddenly found himself with a toddler on his hands. The problem was, the old jaded veteran didn't know how to be a father. He had no experience with the structure nor functioning of a family unit. To him, parents were the type of people who'd take a knife to their infant's eye. Moreover, he lacked the desire to even

attempt to bond with the kid whose failure
dishonored his name.

Only four ages later, Terminus took his
shame to the grave. He died at sea, by Finis's hand, in a fishing accident. He didn't
live to see Finis serve in the Diving Fleet
for two ages as a voluntary adult. He didn't
live to see Finis become a wildly-successful
businessman. Neither did he live to see Finis and his wife, Qui Tsop, give life to the
boy whose military legacy would soon out-
strip his own.

Terminus also never got to witness his
life's work come undone. Back when the
First War was winding down, he'd tasked a
subordinate, a teenager named Oppre Sive,
with authoring the Ichthyo-Conflagrian
Peace Treaty. But, apparently, what Sive
wrote was flawed, leaving the door open to
future conflict. Just as First Earth's Second
World War got spurned by the unreasonable reparations imposed on Germany at the
conclusion of the First World War, Sive's
treaty charged Conflagria with forking over
inordinate quantities of natural resources,
particularly wood. Conflagria did indeed
have more lumber than Ichthyosis—pretty

much any nation on the map did—but, that didn't mean the Island of Fire was lush. It was mostly desert. So, it was impossible for the mages to comply with Sive's demands.

And, so, as the seventh era waned, the System threatened Ichthyosis, once again. The newly-installed Chief of Recruitment, a young diver named Autoero Austere, had little time to find a fleet commander who could walk in Captain Terminus's boots. For ages, Austere and his team acquired child after child, only to be let down time and time again.

At seventeen o'clock on the winter solstice of the seventy-fifth age, Qui Tsop Lechatelierite gave birth to a boy. Austere was dispatched to Krustallos Finire Hospital, within the hour. The general consensus of the recruiting staff was: if not Terminus's son, perhaps his *grand*son could be the one. The Trilateral Committee buzzed with anticipation as Austere went to pick up the baby.

Austere wasn't impressed with what he saw when he arrived at the maternity ward. The Lechatelierite boy appeared to be of the same sickly stature as his grandfather, though there was nothing small about his voice.

Ignoring the desperate cries of his parents, Austere walked out of the hospital with the infant. Cease Terminus Lechatelierite, just hours old, was already the hope of his people.

* * *

As Ichthyosis hunted for its fleet commander, Conflagria searched for its Multi-Source Enchant. However, the System determined that, this time, the war shouldn't necessarily wait for him.

What happened with Spry Scintillate taught the System to be far more skeptical in evaluating potential prophetic candidates. They were quick to dismiss Caitiff Carpus, Spry's grandson, born in the seventy-fourth age alongside his twin sister, Amytal Angel. Caitiff had full wrist magic and a hint of throat spectrum. He was deemed the second partial-multi-sourced mage in history.

Only three ages later, the Second War broke out. And, on July seventh of that very same age, Caitiff Carpus got another sister.

By this time, Spry Scintillate was mostly housebound, on the brink of death from heart disease. Yet, he ventured from his cabin to see his granddaughter on her birthday. He was instantly enchanted by her delicate frame, rosy cheeks, wiry red hair… and, most of all, her brilliant green stare.

Later that afternoon, the girl's Christening Ceremony commenced. The moment the Namers arrived, the baby closed her eyes, refusing to reopen them until all visitors left. Spry could tell that the girl wasn't asleep, either; her breathing was too shallow and uneven. Call him crazy, but the move struck Spry as strategic.

She was given a 'Reserved Name'—one of few set aside for those whose auras were the pinnacles of their colors. Reserved Names were given to the blu*est*, green*est*, yellow*est*, redd*est*—and, so forth—mages of the spectrum. For orange, the special name was 'Tiki.' It had already been given, to none other than Pekoe's son, the newly-installed Principal Tincture. For blue, it was 'Azure.' For green, it was 'Jade.' And, for red, it was 'Scarlet.' Coronate's daughter was Scarlet Carmine July. Despite her low birthweight, her aura was positively radiant. It was so healthy, it scintillated.

Immediately, Spry grew sick with worry. From his rickety wooden wheelchair, he reached with trembling hands to stroke the girl's flaming cheeks. Concentrating hard, he caressed her locks, face and lids. And, in the process, he touched the spectral web itself—as only a mage of his caliber could—and plucked her frequency like a spectrometer, confirming his worst fear: it was stronger than his.

Spry recoiled, sick heart pounding. With every photon in his aura, he hoped and prayed that the System wouldn't notice her extraordinary power, for her sake.

Spry Scintillate died later that week from cardiac arrest, six ages before his granddaughter's Circle Trial.

Sixteen ages before the first rebellion in Conflagrian history.

Made in the USA
Coppell, TX
25 March 2022